Tonight T... No Subterfuge,

no seduction, open or subtle. They simply needed each other and were there to give of themselves and receive in turn.

"Case—" she began softly, succumbing to the urge to express something of what trembled inside her.

"No," he said swiftly, coming over to her and taking her into his arms. She understood at once and complied. He was asking that they have no words tonight, no questions, no explanations or apologies, no promises. Just the unspoken messages their bodies would exchange, messages of passion and love.

CAROLE HALSTON

is the wife of a sea captain, and she writes while her husband is out at sea. Her characters often share her own love of nature and enjoyment of active outdoor sports. Ms. Halston is an avid tennis player and a dedicated sailor.

Dear Reader,

Silhouette Special Editions are an exciting new line of contemporary romances from Silhouette Books. Special Editions are written specifically for our readers who want a story with heightened romantic tension.

Special Editions have all the elements you've enjoyed in Silhouette Romances and *more*. These stories concentrate on romance in a longer, more realistic and sophisticated way, and they feature greater sensual detail.

I hope you enjoy this book and all the wonderful romances from Silhouette.

Karen Solem
Editor-in-Chief
Silhouette Books

CAROLE HALSTON
Something Lost, Something Gained

Silhouette Special Edition
Published by Silhouette Books New York
America's Publisher of Contemporary Romance

SILHOUETTE BOOKS, a Division of Simon & Schuster, Inc.
1230 Avenue of the Americas, New York, N.Y. 10020

ISBN: 0-671-53663-X

First Silhouette Books printing May, 1984

10 9 8 7 6 5 4 3 2 1

Map by Ray Lundgren

Books by Carole Halston

Silhouette Romance

Stand-In Bride #62
Love Legacy #83
Undercover Girl #152
Sunset in Paradise #208

Silhouette Special Edition

Keys to Daniel's House #8
Collision Course #41
The Marriage Bonus #86
Summer Course in Love #115
A Hard Bargain #139
Something Lost, Something Gained #163

For Monty, my husband, ardent supporter, and able captain of all those vessels upon which we have set sail, not least of which was the capricious *Ruth Baby* in the Grenadines . . .

Something Lost, Something Gained

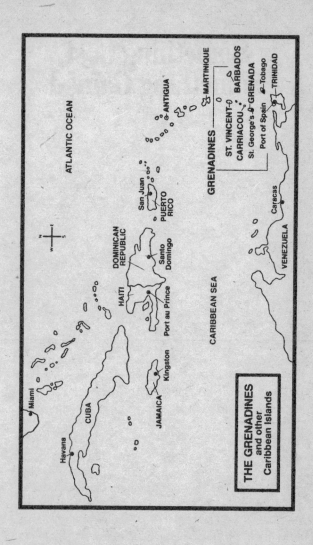

THE GRENADINES
and other
Caribbean Islands

Chapter One

Megan helped herself to a long-stemmed glass of white wine from a linen-draped table and moved away a few feet, letting her gaze rove eagerly over the large room. Everybody who was even remotely "somebody" in the world of women's magazine publishing was expected to be here at this party, along with the throngs of those like herself who hoped to work themselves up into the higher echelons.

It was hard for Megan to believe that *she,* Megan O'Riley Ballantine, was a part of this world at all and was here tonight at a midtown Manhattan hotel with editors whose names were known by nearly every woman in America. After two years of working on the staff of a top women's magazine, Megan's enthusiasm might have been dulled somewhat by certain realities that were difficult to accept, but she still loved the daily challenge of her work, loved the sense of accomplishment in a tough, competitive field.

And whatever she had accomplished thus far in her short career, she could give herself credit for it, not Case, Megan reflected, raising her wine glass to her lips and taking a tiny sip. Those who were present at the party and had some acquaintance with Megan would be surprised to know her name *was* Ballantine. Two years ago when she'd applied for a minor staff position on the big name magazine, never really expecting to be hired, some impulse had guided her to give her maiden name. She hadn't wanted to use Case's reputation as one of the leading fashion photographers, not just in the United States but in the entire world. And after the way he had reacted when he learned she had been offered the job and taken it, she had been doubly glad she hadn't used her married name.

But lately Megan had begun to wonder if she might have to swallow her pride after all and let the fact be known that Case Ballantine was her estranged husband. It came as a bitter pill to Megan that hard work might not be enough, not when others competing for higher positions were willing to use any connection they might have as a lever. If she never got an opportunity to prove herself capable of greater responsibility, what good would her pride do her then?

If Megan were looking for excuses, she could have told herself it wasn't easy starting a career at thirty, as she had done, nor was it easy to commute into the city from Connecticut and divide her energies between her work and the demands of being a mother to two children. Kathleen was twelve now and in the throes of preadolescence. She and her girlfriends considered themselves far too adult and sophisticated to have anything whatever to do with ten-year-old Danny.

"Megan! So here you are! I've been keeping one eye out for you. I *really* hate to be so pushy, but I simply *must* have that readers' survey in my hands by Monday morning, the very *latest!*"

Megan smiled up at the tall, blond young woman and wondered again, as she had wondered how many hundreds of times in her thirty-two years, if tall people didn't automatically have an advantage in life.

"No problem, Val," she assured her colleague on the magazine staff. "I'll have it to you tomorrow afternoon instead. How's that?"

"You're a darling!" Val declared, and having achieved her mission, glanced around the room with appreciative blue eyes. "Say, isn't this a *fabulous* get-together? Everybody—and I do mean *everybody* —is here. Excuse me while I circulate!" She touched Megan on the shoulder, as though to apologize for deserting her for more advantageous contacts, and then glided off.

Megan watched Val as she approached a group clustered around one of the top editors in the country, who listed among her accomplishments a best-selling autobiography outlining her rise to success. Noticing the way Val insinuated herself into the group and worked her way toward the center, Megan had to admire her technique and wish she had more of Val's boldness. Megan should be mingling herself, rubbing elbows with as many important people as possible, the kind of people who could give her the break she needed. Because if hard work wasn't enough and Megan was going to have to compete with the likes of Val—young women in their twenties who were bright, confident, and aggressive—Megan had to play by their rules. Otherwise, she would be overlooked.

Squaring her shoulders and mentally gathering her courage, Megan began to drift through the large, crowded ballroom, stopping to greet and chat briefly with acquaintances. Small-boned and petite with flame-red hair and vivid blue eyes attesting to her Boston Irish heritage, she found herself having to tilt back her head and look up to nearly everyone, in spite of the spike-heeled shoes she wore. But Megan was too intent upon locating one editor in particular to worry about her diminutive size.

Dee Gardner was editor-in-chief of America's leading fashion magazine, *Today's Fashion,* the unchallenged oracle of what colors would be "in" next season, where the hemlines would be, and what was newest and most exciting in designer fashions and smart accessories. According to the trade grapevine, Dee's staff would soon have an opening that Megan secretly longed to have an opportunity to fill: assistant editor of the travel section.

The job would be perfect for her, a respectable

step up the editorial ladder and yet not too high a step for her to manage. She just *knew* she could handle it and handle it well, but so could dozens of others in Megan's present position and with her level of experience. The problem she faced was bringing herself somehow to Dee's attention, singling herself out among her competitors for the job. So far Megan had come up with only one idea for doing that—she could let Dee Gardner know that Case Ballantine was Megan's husband.

As repugnant as the idea was to Megan, as much an affront as it was to her pride, she knew using her marital status would do nobody any harm and possibly herself a lot of good. Megan knew that she wouldn't have any professional influence with Case and wouldn't try to use it even if she did, but once she had the job, she was confident she could prove herself without any further help from him, without any favors. And Megan *was* still married to Case, even if she hadn't seen him or spoken to him face-to-face in two years now. So far, neither of them had taken any steps toward getting a divorce.

If he hadn't been so incredibly pigheaded, so chauvinistic, so *unreasonable* about her need to get out of the house and do something on her own, they wouldn't be separated at all! Megan felt her temper rising and an all-too-familiar swell of frustration as she remembered how adamant Case had been two years ago that she either give up the job she had accepted without his knowledge or give up being his wife. He insisted she couldn't do both. And he had simply *refused* to listen to reason!

Megan had been so furious at first at what she

construed as his callous indifference to her own
needs that she had said a great many things she later
regretted. Then she had tried to point out to Case
that if he forced her to give in to his wishes, she
would be little more than a chattel to him. Her spirit
and her pride would be broken. They wouldn't have
a marriage of equals. But he hadn't been swayed by
anything she said. He had been stubborn, inflexible,
and—Megan felt a stab of pain inside her breast as
honesty compelled her to add, "wounded."

But tonight *wasn't* a time for regret or introspection. What had been done had been done. Megan
firmly shoved to the back of her mind all her
misgivings about the past and about what she had
come here tonight planning to do. Right now she
had to locate Dee Gardner and play it by ear from
there.

When Megan finally caught sight of the editor, she
was surprisingly close, some fifteen or twenty feet
away. A sudden shifting of people left open a direct
path between Megan and Dee Gardner and the
group clustered around her. But all thought of the
much-desired position on Dee's fashion magazine
fled Megan's mind as she stared in disbelief at a
powerfully built bearded man standing next to the
editor, the object of her undivided attention and
conspicuously casual in his attire. In chino slacks and
a black turtleneck, he looked virile and masculine
and unconcerned about the fact that those around
him wore suits and cocktail party finery.

Case! What was he doing here? Megan asked
herself dazedly when she had recovered from that
first shock of seeing him. Desperately she tried to

adjust to the discovery that he was present at the party and that after two years they would see each other, talk to each other—in front of other people. She wasn't surprised that he had been invited, but that he had chosen to attend when he made a point of *never* attending big parties like this one. Hadn't that been one of the bones of contention between him and Megan? She had accused him more than once of being ashamed of her, of not wanting to take her out among the celebrities he worked with, the famous models and actresses known the world over for their stunning looks. It had seemed the height of selfishness to Megan that Case denied her some little taste of the glamour that was common fare in his working life.

But now as Megan gazed at the man who was so familiar to her—so *dear* in spite of the misunderstandings that kept them apart—she knew he wasn't enjoying himself. The shrewd, dark eyes were slightly narrowed in a customary expression as he looked from one person to another, following the rapid-fire conversation but taking little active part in it. A faint polite smile hovered at the corners of his full, sensual mouth. When he was relaxed and genuinely amused, that mouth could broaden into a wide disarming grin.

Suddenly Megan was swamped by emotions. She'd known that eventually she and Case would see each other again. It had been a combination of pride and the fear that she wouldn't be able to stand up to him that had made her avoid contact at first, and then she'd realized he was going to great lengths himself to assure that he wouldn't have to see her, picking up the kids when she wasn't home or arranging to meet them somewhere besides the house. Now that he was standing just a few feet away from her, all their differences seemed so soluble to her. Why should two people who loved each other stay apart when they had shared so much and had so much to offer each other? Surely Case had had time to think and would be more reasonable now. Perhaps he had even come to this party knowing he would probably run into Megan here.

Megan felt her spirits soar at the prospect of reconciliation with Case. It seemed like fate that she had discovered him standing next to Dee Gardner. Megan could join Dee and Case right now. Her relationship to Case could be brought out into the open in the most natural, honest way, and Megan would not be made to feel in the least manipulative or devious.

But what if Case hasn't changed his mind? This unhappy thought made Megan hesitate instead of moving at once to act out the happy scenario she envisioned. In the meanwhile, Case shifted his stance restlessly, his dark eyes roving around the room and coming eventually to Megan. She watched, wide-eyed and mesmerized, as recognition extinguished the cynical gleam in his eyes and the aloofness was replaced by warmth.

He wasn't surprised, Megan noted. He *had* come here expecting to see her. She stayed precisely where she was, passive and waiting, while Case spoke a few words to his companions and then covered the distance between himself and Megan with his light, athletic stride, a holdover from his youthful years in amateur boxing. Some self-protective instinct urged Megan not to submit to that warm possession in Case's face as he came toward her. After two years how could he look at her across a room as though they'd parted just that morning under the most amicable of circumstances? *Had* he changed his thinking and realized he was being unreasonable?

"Hello, Meg."

The simple greeting was spoken in a low, intimate voice that denied the existence of anyone else in the room except for Megan and himself. Case was the only person who'd ever gotten by with calling her the hated nickname, but at nineteen she hadn't been able to summon a wisp of indignation when he spoke it in a tone that made it a caress. He'd used it ever since.

"Case. I certainly didn't expect to see *you* here." The quick, nervous reply had an undertone of desperation. When Case looked down at her with that indulgent, protective way of his, Megan was tempted to go back to him on *any* terms. For one crazy moment she wished she could wipe out the last two years and slip back in time. But that was impossible and she knew it. Giving in to Case would mean relinquishing her own identity, and she'd fought so hard, given up so much, for the right to be herself.

"I hoped I'd run into you," he replied with simple candor, ignoring her efforts at coolness and sensing the agitation she was feeling inside. It evidently had been a shock for her, running into him unexpectedly like this. He hadn't decided until the last minute to come to the party, and his only reason had been to see her. Nothing might be accomplished if that damned job of hers still meant more to her than he did, but he had simply *had* to see her.

Taking her arm, Case manipulated the two of them over to a little island of unoccupied space where they would have a small measure of privacy.

"You look great, Meg," he complimented her, his eyes going over her hungrily and taking in every detail of her beautifully groomed appearance. The chic black dress fit perfectly and flattered her tiny, curvaceous figure, but he thought it made her look too fragile. He liked her better in a gingham shirt and tight jeans. Remembering the way the denim would cling to the shapely curves of her bottom, Case felt a quickening in his groin that made him want to pick her up and carry her out of this huge room of people and straight to the nearest bed. It was agony to remember the way she had *felt* when he would cup her rounded buttocks in his hands and lift her up against him. Two years. God, it seemed more like an eternity to him.

"Thanks," Megan managed, finding Case's inspection profoundly disturbing. Whatever their differences the last few years of their marriage, she and Case had never experienced any problems with sexual incompatibility. He made her feel all woman, and now his blatantly sexual gaze aroused dormant needs at a time when there were more pressing issues to be confronted.

"You're looking good yourself, Case," she said, thinking privately that he looked tired. His dark beard was more heavily peppered with gray than it had been two years ago. "How have you been?"

Case shrugged. Such a simple question and so impossible to answer with a simple reply. He had to go easy. He couldn't just blurt out the way he felt, that something *had* to give with the two of them pretty soon because he couldn't go on much longer with things the way they were in his life.

"Oh, okay, I guess. I've been working a lot." He glanced over toward Dee Gardner.

Megan followed his gaze and saw that the editor was looking in their direction, a speculative expression on her face indicating she had not overlooked their tête-à-tête.

"Why is Dee Gardner so hot on your trail?" Megan asked, guided by intuitive instincts that had become fine-tuned during the past two years. She'd seen the way Dee was dripping honey all over Case.

It required some effort for Case to answer her, simply because Dee Gardner's interest in him was the farthest thing from his mind at the moment. As far as he was concerned, the Dee Gardners of the world shouldn't even have a place in his private life. He only tolerated them for the benefit of those few people in the world who were truly important to him, foremost among them Megan and the two children she had borne him.

"Dee's like a bloodhound when it comes to sniffing out the scent of a big feature," Case replied cynically, expanding Megan's metaphor. His voice was a blend of contempt and reluctant admiration.

Megan listened with a growing sense of ironic disbelief as Case told her briefly and without any enthusiasm whatsoever that he had agreed to do a combination fashion and travel feature for a major

French fashion magazine. The assignment would require him to fly down to the Caribbean. There he would sail aboard a three-masted schooner as it made its way from island to island in the group of Windward Islands known as the Grenadines. He would be photographing one of the most popular top French models in various designer fashions.

"And Dee Gardner wants the same feature for her magazine, too," Megan stated when he had finished.

Something odd in her voice caught Case's attention and put him on the alert.

"Right the first time. Only she doesn't want a translation of the French version. She wants to send her own writer."

"So what bothers you about that?"

Case's eyes narrowed as he studied Megan's abstracted features. The strange something in her voice was still there.

"Nothing, except that I won't agree to it unless it's settled in advance exactly which magazine will be in charge of things—have the last word. Otherwise, the whole thing could turn into a power struggle."

"I'm sure that can be worked out," Megan said slowly, trying to get a grip on her stampeding thoughts. Her heart had begun to pound wildly, causing the blood to rush through her veins. This was all just too much to believe! Here she had come to this party with the vague hope of making some impression on Dee Gardner, only to discover that the big opportunity of her life had materialized and hung within reach. But the person who could pluck that opportunity down within reach of Megan's trembling fingers was, of all people in the world,

Case, her own husband, and the person least likely to want to advance her career.

"Meg, are you all right?" Case's inquiry was sharp with concern. She had gone quite pale underneath the skillfully applied makeup that didn't quite hide the light sprinkling of golden freckles that she detested and he thought were cute.

The worried frown on Case's face helped to boost Megan's courage. Case still cared for her even if he didn't understand her need for an identity apart from his. If she made him understand how much in his power it was to help her, could he refuse her? She *had* to push her pride aside and ask him.

"When I saw you a few minutes ago—talking to Dee Gardner—" Megan began in a halting manner, having to stop and take deep calming breaths, "I was looking for her. I wanted to talk to her, somehow make a good impression on her." Case's eyes had narrowed and his face hardened as Megan talked. A sinking sensation in the pit of her stomach did not bode well for the outcome of her appeal, but she hurried on. "You see, there's an opening coming up on her magazine that I'd give *anything* to get. It would be just *perfect* for me right now. If she knew that I was your wife—"

Megan broke off as the incredulous light in Case's dark eyes changed to that cynical gleam he trained on the rest of the world, not on her. He wasn't going to help her! she realized with a surge of dismay that was more than she could bear for just a second or two, and then a searing rage came to her aid and burned away the disappointment and the pain.

"All I'm asking you is to use your influence to get

me a *chance* to prove myself!" she spat out at him, trying desperately to keep her voice from becoming shrill. She didn't want everyone within thirty feet to hear her. "Is that so much for you to do?"

Case had his hands in his pockets, knotted into hard fists. Unconsciously he had widened his stance. Normally not at all a violent man, he suddenly felt a hot urge to flatten all these people who held such power over Megan that she would humble herself to him as she had just done. He knew what that must have cost her.

"What in God's name do you *need* to prove?" he bit out harshly, trying as she had done to keep his voice low. "As far as I'm concerned, not a damned thing! You're my *wife*, Meg! The mother of my two kids. What is it you want that I can't give you?" Taking in a deep breath, Case managed to bring under control the deep frustration that had been gnawing at him for two long, hellish years. "Why would I do the very thing that would keep you away from me?" In spite of his effort to sound calmly reasoning, he couldn't keep out the suppressed violence, which was directed not at her personally but at circumstances that had turned his life upside down.

Megan couldn't trust herself to speak during a long moment when her wide, angry gaze plumbed his, which was vaguely apologetic and yet utterly implacable. Case was as bullheaded and unreasonable as ever! He wasn't going to lift a finger to help her—and now that she had spilled the beans to him, he could do just the opposite with Dee Gardner. With all her heart and soul, Megan wished there were some way she could retaliate, some way she could force Case to realize just what it felt like to be inside *her* skin this moment. But how could he possibly understand when he was a talented man with an established career?

"Suit yourself, Case Ballantine," she blazed in a shrill, uneven voice that reflected how close she was to losing all control. By now she didn't give a damn if she was attracting attention to them. "But just get one thing through that thick skull of yours. I'm *not* coming crawling back to you whether I ever amount to anything or not. I'm going to keep *working*—" Megan gulped air into her lungs, struggling for control. "I'm going to keep *trying*—"

Case's hands closed around her shoulders and administered a gentle but authoritative shake.

"Meg! Calm down!" he ordered in a stern undertone.

With disconcerting suddenness the spurt of temper was gone, leaving Megan limp and empty and then vulnerable to emotion of a different kind. Now she had to fight against the awful need to break down into sobs, like a child who has been provoked into willfulness but is sorry when the damage has been done. She must *not* weep in front of Case and all these people.

"I'm sorry, Case," she apologized with ragged dignity. "I didn't mean to embarrass you—"

"Damn it, Meg, you didn't embarrass me," he broke in roughly, his fingers moving on her shoulders in a caress whose gentleness belied his gruffness. "I don't give a damn about any of these people. They can think whatever they want to. But I *do* give a damn about you. You're my *wife,* Meg. For God's sake, I don't want you ever 'crawling' back to me, but I do want you back. I miss you. I miss 'us.' I'd like you and me and the kids to be a family again. Does this job of yours still mean more to you than that?"

Megan felt an emotional fatigue stealing through her and was almost grateful, since it helped her to endure the raw pain in Case's voice and in his face. A great sense of hopelessness engulfed her as she realized that, contrary to her fleeting optimism tonight when she first saw Case, nothing had changed between herself and him. Absolutely nothing. He still didn't understand.

"It's still an 'either-or' proposition, isn't it, Case?" she asked wearily. "I can't be your wife and have a career of my own, too. I have to choose." Megan gathered her courage and made a slight shrugging motion, mentally bracing herself for having to stand alone, without the strength and support of Case's clasp on her shoulders. He read her wishes immediately and dropped his hands.

"I'd like nothing more myself than for us to be a family again," she continued sadly but with a kind of resignation. "I love you. And I know you love me, too. But I need something more out of life than being your wife, Case, and the mother of your children. I need something that's *me,* that's apart from you and the kids. Why can't you understand that and accept it?"

"I understand that you're the most important person in the world to me, and that means nothing to you," Case countered bleakly. Inside he was sick with disappointment. "Everything I've ever done has been for us, not for myself. I make more than enough money to take care of my family. You don't *need* to work."

They had followed the well-worn route to the same old impasse that had resulted in their separation two years ago. Once again Megan experienced a familiar uncertainty. Was she wrong in not giving in to Case? He had been a good husband to her, a good father to their children, certainly a good provider after those early, lean years when he had struggled to build his career in photography, happening by chance more than by design to work himself up in fashion photography.

Megan had been a starry-eyed nineteen, too much in love to think of practicality, when they married thirteen years ago. Case at twenty-four was a happy-go-lucky freelance photographer who made enough money to support his modest needs but certainly not enough to take on a family. Even then he hadn't wanted his wife to work. Megan had chided him for being old-fashioned, but secretly she had been disarmed by the additional proof that he loved her. And then when she promptly got pregnant with Kathleen, the matter seemed taken out of her hands. She had stayed behind in Boston, cozily ensconced in a tiny apartment near her parents, while a new, determined Case went off to New York City to build a career for himself in photography.

Among the jobs that had come his way were several taking photographs for the portfolios of aspiring young models. The burly young photographer who looked as if he should be snapping shots at sporting events apparently had displayed a knack for fashion photography that soon got him attention. One assignment had led to another until eventually Case Ballantine was one of the biggest names in the fashion photography business.

As soon as he had been financially able, he had brought Megan and the two children—Danny had been a baby then, arriving two years after Kathleen —from Boston and settled them in Connecticut, safely out of the city. And there he had kept them, in increasing comfort as his income and reputation grew. Always, and sometimes to Megan's discontent, Case had kept his professional and family lives separate, choosing not to attend big, lavish parties to which he was invited and insisting that he would much rather be home than travel to the distant, exotic-sounding places his assignments took him.

Everything had been fine between Megan and Case as long as she accepted the role Case assigned her, wife and mother. But by the time Danny had entered kindergarten, Megan was feeling desperate to get away from her large, beautiful house and do something entirely nondomestic, something that had nothing to do with her family. When she acted upon that urge, the problems between herself and Case had begun.

He couldn't understand why she would sell cosmetics door to door when she didn't need the money, why she would take course after course in everything from business law to creative writing and study hard to do well in them, why it had been such a source of pride to her when she began writing freelance articles and actually sold some of them to magazines and newspapers. Finally his patience had snapped when he came home from a European assignment and learned Megan had applied for and gotten a job in the city, working for a big women's magazine. She had to make up her mind, he'd demanded, between him and the job. Now, after two years, he hadn't changed his mind.

Did that mean he would never change it? This possibility brought ice to Megan's heart. Seeing him tonight and talking to him had made her remember so much that was good about their marriage, so much that she didn't want to give up forever. She missed his companionship, his lovemaking, the feeling of being cherished and loved. She also bore a heavy sense of responsibility for having denied her children the constant presence of their father.

Should Megan give in? Should she sacrifice her need to accomplish something on her own for the benefit of her children and her husband? *Could* she go back to Case now and be what he wanted her to be? These were all questions Megan would have to answer, but not now, not tonight with the air between herself and Case so filled with raw emotion. And a movement in the periphery of her vision made Megan glance over to see that Dee Gardner was detaching herself from her companions with every intention of tracking Case down. The editor would soon be upon them, no doubt bursting with curiosity.

"I *do* need to work, Case," she said hurriedly, aware that she had little time to get said what she needed to say to him before she fled. "Not for money, perhaps, but for other reasons I'm afraid you will never understand. It just seems there's no solution for us. Unless one of us gives in to the other, we'll have to go on living apart and not being happy with the situation."

Megan blinked hard. The damned tears were about to take over again, and Dee Gardner was definitely headed their way now.

"I'm just not sure we can ever go back," she almost whispered. "I don't know if I can live the rest of my life waiting home for you to come and tell me about all the exciting places you've gone, the famous people you've worked with and talked to. I used to feel that I was living on the outskirts of life. Now, at least I'm *experiencing* things firsthand for myself—"

"Case, you naughty fellow! Why did you run off like that when we have so much to talk about?"

Dee Gardner sent her voice ahead of her when she was within six or eight feet of them. Case snapped his head around in her direction, his frown anything but welcoming. Megan took advantage of his momentary transfer of attention and slid away, hoping with all her heart he wouldn't come after her. She couldn't take much more, not tonight.

Making straight for the exit, Megan left the party, her sensation of panic gradually quieting when it became obvious that Case wasn't in pursuit. Then, paradoxically, there followed a feeling of letdown and disappointment that he hadn't come after her.

She carried in her mind a vivid image of the way Case had looked toward the last. He had been skeptical—or perhaps *bewildered* was more accurate —when Megan admitted how she envied him all the opportunities his job afforded him to do and experience what was so totally removed from the lives of ordinary people. Hadn't she made it clear to him for years that she thirsted for the glamour and the excitement that he took for granted?

Later in the evening when Megan had had time for her emotions to settle, time to go over all that had occurred, she was anything but pleased with herself for the way she had handled the surprise encounter with Case. When was she ever going to learn to control that temper of hers? When was her head going to rule her emotions? She couldn't expect Case to take her seriously as a career woman if she spat at him like a shrew instead of discussing their differences in an intelligent, rational manner.

Megan resolved that she would not let matters between them just drop until the next surprise encounter. She would make it her business to call Case and make some arrangement for them to meet in privacy and hash out their differences. Perhaps he would even consent to professional counseling. An objective, outside view might be helpful to both of them.

Even as she made these firm resolves, telling herself there *was* hope of salvaging her marriage without giving up her right to a career of her own, Megan feared deep down that she was only deluding herself. The past two years she had lived with the basic optimism that she and Case would work out their differences, would get back together again. After tonight, though, she was afraid he might never accept her as she was. And in the clear light of reason, Megan knew she wouldn't be able to fit herself into the mold Case wanted. It simply wouldn't work, even if she tried.

And yet, how could she be happy without Case, knowing that he was not happy either? There seemed no solution.

Chapter Two

*M*egan felt anything but her best the next morning. She had had difficulty falling asleep and then when she finally did, she had slept poorly. The first hour and a half at work, it seemed to her there were hundreds of people making demands upon her. By ten o'clock she had a dull, throbbing headache and had to struggle to sound pleasant and cheerful.

"Hello," she spoke into the telephone receiver, when the lighted button on the console accompanied by that irritating space-age sound told her she had yet another call, the umpteenth one in the last fifteen minutes. "Megan O'Riley here."

"Megan, Dee Gardner speaking," came a familiar

throaty smoker's voice. "Would you be free to have lunch with me today?"

Between the time Megan's mouth went lax with astonishment and she was able to summon speech, all her fatigue and irritation fled, to be replaced by the most intense curiosity shot with alternating strains of hope and skepticism. Had Megan's work come to Dee's attention? No, that was hardly likely. Then, had Case relented and spoken a word in Megan's behalf to the editor of the nation's top fashion magazine? Had he agreed to do the big Caribbean feature for Dee as well as for the French magazine if she would give Megan a crack at the assistant editor's job?

No, Megan quickly discounted that possibility, too. Case had been adamant in his refusal to do anything to help Megan along in her career. Last night she hadn't even gotten far enough in her request to specify what job was open.

The only reasonable interpretation of the unexpected invitation to lunch was curiosity on Dee's part. She had noted the emotional tête-à-tête between Megan and Case last night and probably wanted to get to the bottom of it. If she discovered Megan to have some influence with the well-known fashion photographer, Dee wouldn't hesitate to try to make use of it. She wanted that big Caribbean feature for her magazine and would get it any way she could.

If Megan's analysis of the editor's motivations was accurate, she would be faced with the same decision she had evaded last night when she left the party early. Should she reveal her relationship to Case?

Somewhat to her own surprise, Megan discovered she no longer had any qualms about letting it be known that she was Case Ballantine's wife. But at the same time she also knew she would make it unmistakably clear that Case did not approve of her career and that she would not have any professional influence with him.

Having firmly made up her mind, Megan looked forward to the luncheon without any of that mental discomfort that uncertainty breeds, only to discover that she wasn't as prepared as she thought she was. Still another surprise was in store.

The restaurant Dee had chosen was tucked away in one of the older hotels and noted for its quiet, discreet atmosphere. They were shown to a booth along one paneled wall and given menus to study. Megan glanced at hers, realizing that she was hungry and looking forward to a good meal in this restful atmosphere. If things went according to her expectations, she and Dee would just talk general shop for a while before Dee got around to digging for the information she wanted.

Suddenly Megan was aware of Dee's intent regard and looked up from her menu to find the other woman watching her with all the concentrated patience of a German shepherd about to pounce on a rabbit that had hopped unsuspectingly out of its cage.

"I'll just be honest with you right from the start, Megan," the editor stated without any preamble. "I'd feel better sending a more experienced writer. But if I have to gamble in order to get that feature, then I will."

Megan blinked, feeling slightly foolish as she tried to fathom Dee's meaning. The feature she was referring to was probably the one Case had mentioned last night, but who was the inexperienced writer Dee would "gamble" on? Certainly not *herself!*

Dee eyed Megan's bewildered countenance with some skepticism for several seconds and then apparently decided that nobody could be that good an actress.

"Don't tell me you don't know," she said chidingly, but not without kindness. "Surely that's what that heated discussion between you and Case was about last night at the party? After you made your dramatic exit, Case let me know in no uncertain terms that the only way he would do the feature for me was if I hired you and sent you along as the American writer."

Megan struggled to assimilate the astounding information Dee had just delivered with all apparent seriousness. Last night when Case was telling her about his latest assignment, it *had* run through her mind that she would love to be the American writer for Dee's magazine and that Case had enough clout to get the choice assignment for her. But she hadn't really *seriously* thought it was a possibility. More within the realm of everyday reality had been the hope that Dee might give Megan a chance at the assistant editor's job in return for Case's agreeing to do the Caribbean feature for both magazines. The prospect of flying down to the Caribbean and cruising from tropical island to tropical island on a sailing schooner was too much for Megan's mind to grasp, not to mention working with one of France's top fashion models.

"I really *didn't* know," Megan murmured, aware that she was being anything but blasé and sophisticated. She was too besieged with questions to even think straight, but before she could sort them out according to priority, Dee was taking a cigarette from her monogrammed leather case and proceeding to outline Megan's future in a matter-of-fact manner.

"You'll want to give notice right away and come over to work on my staff." She lighted her cigarette and took a deep draw, continuing after she had expelled the cloud of smoke. "I told Case straight out that I don't carry any deadheads. You'll have a chance to prove yourself with this feature. If you can handle it, there'll be a future for you with my magazine. I won't promise anything more than that."

Megan squared her shoulders under the uncompromising bluntness.

"That's all I ask for from anybody," she replied with dignity. "A chance to prove my ability."

The waiter, who had tried to approach their booth earlier and been peremptorily waved away by Dee, came now and took their orders. Megan's appetite had vanished but she ordered the salad she had decided upon earlier, wondering all the time how to go about phrasing the question that loomed huge in her mind. Had Case told Dee he was married to Megan? It was surprising that the editor hadn't mentioned that reason for his stipulation that Megan be given the writing assignment.

"Did Case explain to you why . . ." Megan began awkwardly and then was stilled by a hard, knowing look that Dee emphasized by crushing out her cigarette butt. The look told Megan what she'd wanted to know. Case hadn't told Dee he was Megan's husband. The editor clearly assumed that Case and Megan were having an affair, and he was doing a favor for his girlfriend.

Under the circumstances it was probably highly irrational for Megan to feel the sense of injury that she did. After all, she was the one who had originally concealed her married name. Why should she resent Case for not telling Dee the secret Megan had so carefully kept? But resent him she did, and the emotion brought with it a surge of renewed determination to succeed. She *would* take this opportunity Case had given her and prove her ability. She *would* be somebody on her own.

It pleased Megan to note the change in Dee Gardner's manner by the time they had finished lunch and discussed the plans for the Caribbean feature at some length. The editor obviously felt more optimistic about her new employee's chance for success with her challenging assignment. During the three-month interval between now and the first of December, when she would be flying down to the Caribbean to do the feature on location, Megan planned to do everything she could to impress Dee with her diligence and potential.

Megan would have been surprised if she had read Dee's mind toward the last. It rankled a little that Dee had been forced to allow Case Ballantine to bully her into hiring his pint-sized little redheaded girlfriend. Dee didn't like being bullied by anyone. But if she was any judge of character at all—and in her line of work she had to be—she would predict that Case might have his hands full with this assignment, in more ways than one. Megan O'Riley had spirit and brains and probably a temper to go with her hair color. Case Ballantine would learn the hard way to keep his personal and professional lives separate.

That same afternoon Megan gave notice and created a buzz of excitement as the news got out that she was changing over to Dee Gardner's magazine. For the time being, though, she kept to herself the really big news, her assignment to the Caribbean feature.

All her efforts to get in touch with Case met with failure. He didn't answer the telephone at his apartment, and his answering service would admit to no knowledge of his whereabouts. Megan experienced a growing sense of frustration as a week passed and then another, and she had no opportunity to thank Case for the big boost he had given her and to question him about his reasons for changing his mind. Surely he must know she was bursting to talk to him!

Then on a Friday evening, Megan answered the telephone without any premonition that the caller was Case.

"Hello, Meg," came his deep, familiar voice. "Do the kids have plans this weekend? I thought I'd pick them up in the morning if they don't."

"Case!" Megan's surprise was mixed with the exasperation she had experienced in not being able to contact him. "Where have you been?"

As soon as the words were out she wished that she could retract them and make her inquiry in a different tone, one that didn't sound so much like an indignant wife.

"I've called your apartment a hundred times," she added quickly in a lighter key. "Naturally I wanted to thank you for—"

"You must have talked with Dee Gardner," Case cut in, sounding not exactly brusque but not patient either. "I take it she's decided to hire you."

Megan was taken aback by the detachment in his words and also the implication that up until this moment he hadn't known what his remarks to Dee Gardner at the party had set into motion.

"Yes, she has," Megan answered thoughtfully. "Case, where've you been the last two weeks? Did you go on a vacation? You really should let me know . . ." Her voice drifted off on a note of faint reproach that she thought was fully justified.

"I took a couple of weeks off and went back to Boston." There was a pause Megan couldn't read. "Visited some of my old haunts, looked up some people. Sorry if I caused you any concern on my account. You're right, I should have let you know how to get in touch with me in case something came up with the kids."

Megan gritted her teeth and counted slowly to ten. Here she had been so eager to talk to Case, to thank him, to discuss the trip in December, and when she finally got him on the telephone, he acted as if he wasn't even interested in talking to her! Well, she *wouldn't* lose her temper, she *would* thank him, and he *would* tell her why he'd used his influence with Dee Gardner in her behalf.

"Case, I *am* grateful to you. I'm so looking forward to the trip down to the Caribbean. It's like a dream come true!" The determination in Megan's voice had changed to lilting enthusiasm. She couldn't think about that trip without getting excited! "But why did you talk to Dee? You said—"

"What difference does it make?" Case interrupted again. "The important thing is that I did. You got what you wanted, didn't you?"

His tone didn't encourage any further delving into his reasons, but Megan clung stubbornly to her intention.

"But I want to know." The petulance of the demand was heavily laced with disappointment. Case was telling her a great deal more than his actual words stated: Whatever he had done in her behalf, he hadn't changed his attitude one whit.

"It was the least I could do," Case said finally, after a long, heavy silence during which Megan imagined that she could sense a struggle going on at the other end of the line. "Maybe I'm hoping I can make up to you a little for all those wasted years you sat home and waited for me to return from my glamorous travels."

Megan flinched under the bitterness.

"Case, they *weren't* wasted years!" she denied in exasperation. "I didn't say that! I said—" With a loud sigh, Megan broke off, realizing the futility of trying to explain what she *had* meant. At the moment all those recently formed resolutions to meet with Case and iron out their problems seemed like a pipe dream. Suddenly Megan wasn't nearly so elated over her new job and the wonderful prospects for her career.

"I'll get the kids and let you talk to them," she said dully. "They can tell you for themselves what they'd like to do this weekend."

She laid the telephone receiver down before she could hear Case speak her name in a tone urgent with apology and regret and then mutter a string of curses aimed at himself and at the universe in general.

Later in the evening when Megan had recovered somewhat from the plunge her high spirits had taken, she felt more optimistic as she thought of the Caribbean assignment two and a half months away. She and Case would be working together on that and would of necessity have to spend time in each other's company. Surely in two weeks of proximity in such a romantic setting they would come to a new understanding. Megan was counting on it.

Chapter Three

Seated next to Case on the big jet headed for Miami, Megan marveled that the three months had passed so quickly, somehow all the preparations had been made, and the much-anticipated trip to the Caribbean was about to become a reality. She tried to conceal from Case the turmoil seething inside her. One moment she was so filled with elation she could hardly sit still, and then the next she was seized with fits of anxiety as she went over and over in her mind the arrangements she had made for the children. Her mother had willingly come from Boston to stay with them, but her mother was almost sixty now. Her nerves weren't what they used to be. If some emergency occurred, would she be able to take care of it? The Caribbean was a long way away . . .

"Relax," Case ordered mildly, covering her tightly clasped hands with one of his and giving a reassuring squeeze. "The kids will be fine. Grandma O'Riley will have them spoiled rotten by the time you get back. You'll have to listen to a week or two of 'But *Grandma* let us.'"

Megan sighed ruefully, relaxing against the back of her seat. What was the use of trying to hide her feelings from Case, especially her maternal feelings? He knew her too well. Somehow his reassurance that all would be well eased her anxiety and allowed her to focus on the present.

She couldn't have chosen a more desirable companion for this trip than Case. He had the look and easy manner of a seasoned traveler, which of course he was by now. Somewhat to Megan's surprise, he wore a beautifully tailored navy blazer and even a striped tie. She had expected more casual attire and inspected him at first with raised eyebrows.

"Didn't want to embarrass you," he said with a little shrug, understanding at once, and then added, "There are always a few places, even in the tropics, that are sticklers about proper attire. It's easier to wear a jacket than pack it."

"Now we get to the *true* explanation," Megan had teased, her eyes going over him admiringly. Case looked good in well-cut clothes like those he wore. His shoulders were broad in proportion to his waist and hips, and he carried himself with an air of casual confidence. Megan couldn't fail to notice in the airport that women's eyes were drawn to him. At thirty-eight, his dark beard heavily mingled with gray and little lines fanning out from the corners of his penetrating eyes attesting to experience, Case was an attractive man, secure in his masculinity. He would never have a problem finding female companionship wherever he went, Megan reflected with a mixture of pride and jealousy.

It was alluring to speculate that this trip was only the first of many they would take together to far-off glamorous places. The children could survive a few weeks here and there without her. Money wasn't really a problem any more, either . . .

"The others will beat us by several hours." Case's matter-of-fact cadences broke into her rosy daydream, reminding her of the real circumstances of this trip. She was a writer on an assignment, not a vacationing wife.

"You said they would be traveling on a chartered jet from France." Megan heard the dreamy note in her voice and met Case's quick glance a little sheepishly.

"By the way, has anyone mentioned that you and I are the only Americans?" he asked almost brusquely. "You'll be hearing a lot of French spoken, you know."

It was on the tip of Megan's tongue to say she didn't care *what* language was spoken. The thought of hearing strangers carry on fluent conversations in a foreign tongue only heightened her sense of adventure. She had never traveled outside of the United States before. In the interest of harmony Megan curbed the impulse to blurt out these feelings and risk reminding Case of those remarks she had made at the party that night three months ago about waiting home for him all those years when he was traveling to interesting places. Instead she attempted to question him about the other members of the group with whom she would be working.

"What's Marcelle like? You've worked with her before, haven't you?"

Case started to answer her and then checked himself.

"Why don't you wait and form your own impressions?" he suggested.

Megan was frankly miffed at first that he wouldn't share his personal opinion of the French model. Then she had to remind herself again that she and Case were traveling together not as man and wife but as two professionals with jobs to do. Maybe Case had been trying to remind her of that, too.

"You're right," she said coolly. "I should form my own impressions and not rely on yours. You have your job to do, and I have mine. Don't worry, Case, I won't be expecting any extra consideration from you. As far as I'm concerned, nobody has to know we've even known each other before."

Case muttered an obscene expletive under his breath, but when he spoke, his voice was calm.

"I just thought it would be better if I didn't prejudice you, that's all. And you don't have to keep reminding me that you're going along to do a job and not as my wife. I'm well aware of that fact."

Megan opened her mouth to deny that her intention had been to remind him of any such thing, but then she bit back the words, knowing she would only get involved in another fruitless argument with him. There was no further conversation between them during the remainder of the flight to Miami, where they had to board another plane to Barbados.

When they had settled into their places and the second flight was underway, Megan took out a guidebook she knew almost by heart and began flipping through the pages and skimming over the information that the Grenadine Islands were in the chain of islands curving from Puerto Rico to Venezuela. They were a haven for yachtsmen and those who were seeking the "barefoot life," offering some of the best sailing and snorkeling in the world. The variety of plant life was astounding and beautiful, the water crystal clear with a great variety of exotic fish and coral formations, the temperatures warm year round.

"St. Vincent is called the Breadfruit Isle," she informed Case, regardless of the fact that he was deeply engrossed in a highly technical article in a photography magazine. The enthusiasm was bubbling up again in Megan. She wanted to share it with Case and also erase any lingering traces of hard feelings from their exchange on the previous flight.

"Says here Captain Bligh brought the first breadfruit tree from Tahiti and apparently it really took hold. Breadfruit is an important food staple." Megan paused and looked thoughtfully puzzled. "Hard to imagine what a breadfruit would look like, isn't it?" she asked impishly, wrinkling up her pert nose in the way Case adored. "I'm seeing a loaf in cellophane dangling from a limb!"

Megan met his eyes long enough to reassure herself that he wasn't still angry with her and then let her gaze race on down the page of the guidebook.

"And Kingstown is supposed to have a market on Saturday that's something to see," she continued eagerly. "People come from all over the island, some of them by carts pulled by donkeys, and sell their vegetables and fruits. There's also the weekly loading of the banana boats . . ."

Feeling Case's intent gaze, Megan glanced up and caught his expression. Before he could say what he was obviously thinking, she snapped the guidebook closed and sighed.

"There isn't going to be time to see all this, is there?" she said pensively. "We're not on a holiday but a working assignment—isn't that what you were about to say?" A trace of irritation crept in toward the last.

"Precisely," Case stated firmly. "There'll be time to see and do a certain amount, but nine times out of ten on a trip like this, you're too tired by the time you get around to doing anything not absolutely required in the line of duty."

Megan suppressed the urge to disagree with him, keeping to herself the inner certainty that *she* didn't intend to waste a single precious second of this exciting trip. Sure it was work, the kind of work she couldn't get too much of.

The airport at Barbados was minuscule compared to those in New York and Miami, but it was new and modern. For the first time in her limited flying experience, Megan had to deplane right out in the open and walk into the terminal. The novelty compounded her sense of newness and exploration.

However, she wasn't prepared for the smallness of the little plane they boarded to take them from Barbados to St. Vincent. The single cabin held at the most thirty or forty passengers. When they took off into the air, it seemed to Megan that the engine sounds were deafeningly loud. Once airborne, they were jarred and buffeted by air currents. In spite of her desire to be brave, Megan found herself clutching Case's arm when the plane dropped unexpectedly.

"Do you think these pilots are qualified?" she asked in a quavering voice.

"I'm sure they have to be," Case assured her, giving the small hand gripping his sleeve a comforting pat and fighting the urge to put an arm around her and hug her close. "Look down there," he bade, leaning over and gazing through the small window down at the ocean below. "See those little white triangles? Those are yachts under sail. In a couple of days we'll be down there ourselves and people flying overhead will be looking down at us like this."

His efforts at distraction were successful. Megan peered down at the huge expanse of blue. The sailboats he had pointed out were so tiny from this elevation, so vulnerable they might have been miniature toys. Megan couldn't begin to imagine herself down there on one of them. Suddenly being up here in the noisy, bumpy airplane seemed safer than it had before. She felt much calmer.

Still it was a relief to exit from the plane at the St.

Vincent airport and walk on solid ground. The terminal building was low and dingy and incredibly small. They had to stand in line and present their passports to customs officers in dazzling white starched uniforms generously draped with gold braid. Megan suddenly realized that she was truly standing on foreign soil and about to enter a different world.

When they had cleared customs and passed through double doors into a hallway, a wiry, deeply suntanned man roughly Case's height stepped forward and addressed them. His longish hair and full beard were as black as his eyes, which were lit with a friendly twinkle. His casual manner matched his attire, baggy tan shorts and a white T-shirt.

"Monsieur Ballantine?"

"Case Ballantine," Case corrected cordially, taking the Frenchman's hand and shaking it. "Captain Jacques Renard?"

"Jacques," the other man countered, indicating his approval of Case's preference for informality.

When Megan was introduced, she found herself utterly captive to the famous French charm she had heard so much about but never experienced. Jacques didn't kiss her hand but he inclined his head over it in a graceful gesture and made her name sound like music.

"If you will come with me, I have a taxi waiting," Jacques announced in his easy, accented English.

In the taxi Megan found herself sitting next to Case in the backseat while Jacques sat in front with the driver. She had meant to verify her assumption that he was the captain of the sailing schooner chartered for the feature, but there was so much to see outside the windows of the taxi that she paid no attention to the conversation between the two men on the ride from the airport to their destination, whatever that was.

St. Vincent was truly a tropical paradise! Everywhere Megan looked she saw the lushest possible green vegetation spangled with huge vivid blossoms. Flowering vines spilled over nearly every wall and fence, giving charm to the most humble abode. Off to their right were breathtaking glimpses of sapphire-blue water, and every turn in the narrow, twisting road made Megan wish she had a camera to capture the vista. To heighten her exhilaration the taxi seemed to be hurtling along at a high speed, the driver blasting his horn every few seconds to warn those out of sight around a curve.

All too soon, as far as she was concerned, the taxi had come to a stop near a wooden pier extending out into the water. Megan tumbled out of the taxi and gazed around her with an emotional pitch approaching rapture. Everything was as wonderful, as beautiful, as exciting as she had hoped it would be. Her spirit was reaching out and embracing all of the experience.

"Over there is Young Island," Jacques was saying as he pointed across a narrow strip of water. Megan feasted her eyes on greenness separated from the blue water by a white sand beach. From this distance she could see the feathery fronds of palm trees and splashes of color that were clusters of flowers. Nestled into the steep hillsides were cottages. She could make out the angled rooflines and imagine the view from their windows and little front balconies.

Jacques was still talking, but Megan failed to concentrate on his words, bringing her attention back just in time to hear ". . . the *Marie Antoinette.*" Looking in the same direction as the men, she saw among the dozen or so yachts anchored out from shore a gorgeous black-hulled boat, larger than any of the others, with three masts and old-fashioned rigging. The schooner they would be sailing on! Megan stared at it, excitement building in her breast. She would actually be living on that lovely vessel for the better part of two weeks. What an experience of a lifetime!

Giving careful attention to the placement of her feet, Megan followed Jacques along the wooden pier and accepted his help down into a small boat he referred to as a "dink." Case got down into the boat, too, and sat next to her. Hoping not to appear as uneasy as she felt, Megan clung to her side of the boat with a white-knuckled hand as Jacques started the outboard and then headed out across the water.

"Okay?" came a low inquiry, close to her ear.

Megan turned her head and met Case's dark eyes, warming to the smiling reassurance.

"Fine," she assured bravely, finding to her surprise that she really *was* okay. Case wouldn't let anything harmful happen to her.

The small interchange took only a few seconds, but Megan was aware suddenly of a change in the sound of the outboard. They were slowing down, coming up beside a boat with a royal-blue hull and *l'Esprit* written in flowing script on the side. Bewildered, Megan sat there looking from Jacques to Case as they both stood and held the small boat snugly against the larger one.

"You first," Case instructed, nodding at the stainless steel boarding ladder hanging over the side.

Megan did as she was bade, climbing up to the side deck and then stepping carefully down into a large cockpit. Case followed immediately behind her, but Jacques headed the small boat back toward the small pier they had just left.

"He's gone for the luggage," Case explained in reply to the sharp question in Megan's expression.

"But—" she burst out, meaning to ask what was going on. At that moment a pretty young woman with long brown braids appeared in the open hatchway, smiling shyly. As suntanned as Jacques, she wore a printed bikini top and brief white shorts.

"Bonjour," she greeted them in a slightly apologetic manner. "Alina," she enunciated slowly, pointing to herself by way of introduction.

Megan inferred at once that the young woman did not speak fluent English as Jacques did. Taking a cue from Alina, Megan pointed to herself. "Megan," she pronounced distinctly and then pointing to Case, spoke his name.

"Welcome aboard," Alina said slowly, sounding out each syllable carefully, evidently having practiced the courtesy in advance. Her next words were identifiable to Megan only as an offer of some kind.

"She's asking if we would like something cold to drink," Case explained, much to Megan's surprise. "Oui, merci," he said courteously to Alina.

"I didn't know you could speak French!" Megan blurted when Alina had murmured something and disappeared down inside the yacht again.

Case was taking off his jacket and stripping off the tie, which he stuffed in a jacket pocket. Next he unbuttoned the cuffs of his long-sleeved shirt and rolled back the sleeves to the elbow.

"I don't really 'speak' French," he said easily, relaxing back on a cockpit cushion and gesturing for Megan to do the same. "I just know a few basic words and phrases. I can understand more than I can say. Can't wait to get into some more comfortable clothes," he commented, running his fingers around the inside of his shirt collar.

Megan was reminded of the questions she had been about to ask seconds ago when Alina had appeared to distract her.

"Why did Jacques bring us to this boat? Instead of out to the schooner?"

Case looked surprised.

"Haven't you been listening? You and I are staying here aboard Jacques's boat with him and Alina, not on the schooner."

"I don't understand why—" Megan began to protest on a sharp note and then broke off as Jacques came alongside in the dinghy and cut off the outboard motor. Case got up immediately and went over to give him a hand with the luggage, but Jacques refused any help in taking the luggage down inside the boat.

"I can manage," he insisted, waving Case back to his seat in the cockpit before he disappeared as Alina had earlier.

"Now explain what you're talking about," Megan demanded in a low tone so that the French couple wouldn't hear. "Why aren't we staying on the schooner with the others?"

Case met the suspicion in her eyes with a slight frown, but his explanation was patient.

"There isn't room for everybody on the schooner. Marcelle has to have a separate dressing room, and the outfits take up a lot of room, too. This arrangement suits me better anyway. I'd rather not have to stay on the same boat with the others. Working with them all day will be more than enough personal contact. And as Jacques explained in the taxi—when you apparently weren't paying any attention—we needed the smaller yacht along anyway and might as well make use of its accommodations. I'll have to take pictures of the schooner under sail from a distance plus some close-ups of Marcelle lounging on deck."

Megan nibbled at her lower lip, gazing out at the black-hulled vessel anchored out in deeper water.

"I was looking forward to staying on the schooner," she said stubbornly. "It's so beautiful . . . and bigger." The last two words were barely audible and saved her from feeling the brunt of Case's impatience as he realized that for all Meg's excitement over the trip, now that she was actually here she was experiencing some trepidations very understandable under the circumstances. A city girl who had never set foot on a sailboat before, she would be thinking

Jacques's sixty-five-foot ketch was small, when by cruising standards it was actually quite large.

"You've got to realize, Meg, what the others are probably thinking about you and me," Case warned, the gruffness softened by sympathy. "You're not a well-known writer like Cecile is in her country, which causes people to jump to the conclusion that you got this assignment because you're my girl-friend. They also assume we'll be sleeping together." Megan's head snapped around toward Case, but before she could say anything, he hurried on, want-ing to get everything out in the open before Jacques and Alina came up to join them. No doubt they were down there waiting for the two Americans to get their discussion over with. "Besides that misconcep-tion, it was taken for granted also that you would prefer to be quartered with your countryman, for the sake of the others as well as yourself. They all speak French, you remember."

Megan's head was buzzing with a whole set of new questions she didn't know how to ask. Case had said it was a "misconception" that the two of them would be sleeping together. Was he trying to warn her in advance not to expect any sexual intimacy between them even if they were "quartered" together, what-ever that meant?

"How many 'bedrooms' does this boat have any-way?" she asked with elaborate casualness.

Case tensed.

"On a boat it's either 'cabins' or 'staterooms,'" he corrected briefly, his eyes not quite meeting hers. "And don't worry. There are three private state-rooms on this yacht, each one with its own 'head,' or bathroom. You'll have a stateroom of your very own." During the pause that followed, Megan could see that his teeth were clamped so tightly together that his jawline worked under the full beard. When he turned his head suddenly toward her and she could see the emotion in his dark eyes, she was taken aback at the anger and resentment and something else she could only identify as shame. "It isn't usually necessary for me to manipulate a woman into my bed," he added with barely suppressed savagery and immediately regretted the remark, which he recognized for what it was, partly defense and partly retaliation for her unfounded suspicion of his motives. He was human, damn it! If only she knew the irony of her insinuation that he couldn't wait to get her in his bed. God knows, he wanted her, but he was scared of what might happen.

Megan tightened her lips to control their quiver. Now she understood that shame in Case's eyes. At least he had the human decency to feel some guilt when he outright admitted to her he had been going to bed with other women. The thought cut through Megan like a knife, even though intellectually she had known there *would* be other women for him in the course of two years. He was too virile and attractive not to have more than his rightful share of offers. If Megan hadn't come along on this trip, for all she knew he might have been "quartered" with the French writer or even the high fashion model, Marcelle.

"I'm not worried—about anything," Megan muttered in a defensive little voice, knowing full well he could see how jealous she was.

Case said nothing because he couldn't think of anything he *could* say now without getting into explanations that would reveal too much. A man has his pride after all.

When the silence in the cockpit had stretched out uninterrupted for a minute or so, Jacques and Alina must have judged it safe to come out. They emerged with tall glasses of fruit juice and rum for the four of them.

The French couple must be feeling as though they were entering a battle zone, Megan reflected with dismay and embarrassment. Why did she and Case end up arguing every time they got together now? It hadn't always been that way. With a sudden flash of insight she realized the explanation. Case was the one who had changed, not Megan, who had been a spitfire her entire life, quick to lose her temper and pick a fight with the closest person. In the past Case had always refused to argue with her. He would simply state his point of view and say nothing more until Megan's ire had cooled and she could discuss the matter calmly and see things in perspective. What had happened to change Case from a cool, utterly self-contained man to one who lost his temper and visibly seethed with frustration? Megan found that question profoundly disturbing.

With an effort she made herself concentrate on the conversation. Jacques was saying that he would take Case and Megan over to Young Island that evening in the dinghy. There they would meet Marcelle and her retinue and have cocktails in the Young Island hotel bar. Later they would dine in the restaurant. Jacques and Alina would not be joining the party but planned to have dinner ashore on the St. Vincent side. They were close friends with the owners of the Harbor Light restaurant, one of several restaurants on the edge of the water and facing Young Island.

At this point Megan stopped listening once again, the conversation turning to Jacques's experiences in cruising and not directly concerning the arrangements relating to the magazine feature. Mention of the evening's plans had fully revived her anticipation, and she forgot everything else in the absorbing contemplation of what she should wear that night. The lingering traces of regret and annoyance dissipated as she mentally reviewed the contents of her suitcase.

What fun this trip was going to be! she exulted, gazing over at the lush greenness and white beach of Young Island. This was more like a movie than reality. Here she sat on a beautiful yacht, sipping rum punch and looking forward to an evening of cocktails and dinner on a tropical island with a world-famous French model. Megan was finally going to the ball, figuratively speaking, after years of sitting home and dreaming of being there. She planned to savor every glamorous second of the experience!

Chapter Four

$\mathcal{N}$ight was falling softly when Jacques took Case
and Megan over to Young Island in the dinghy. The
western sky was still streaked with faint pinks and
lavenders, die-hard remnants of the flamboyant
tropical sunset Megan had found too beautiful to
believe real. A breeze ruffled the surface of the
darkening water and caressed her bare shoulders and
back. Megan shivered pleasurably, glad she had
brought along the light cardigan she carried over one
arm.

While Jacques held the small boat close to the
wooden pier, Case stepped ashore and then helped
Megan out. She bent and slipped her feet into
low-heeled sandals, as excited as a high school girl

about to make her entrance at the prom. Megan felt good about the ankle-length halter dress. The gay floral print suited the gaiety of her mood, and the fabric was one of those wrinkle-free cotton-and-polyester blends. If she had any regret about her appearance, it was the porcelain whiteness of her skin, and yet she knew that wasn't likely to change, even though she had optimistically brought along a highly recommended suntan cream and intended to work on a suntan.

They didn't have far to walk to the hotel bar, whose entire front was open, facing onto the water. The other members of the feature crew were already there when Case and Megan arrived. She was busy the first ten minutes meeting everyone and registering so many impressions that her head reeled.

"Case, *cherie! Quelle plaisir!*" greeted a thin, nervous brunet woman about Megan's age. She stepped forward holding out both hands to Case and lifting her face for him to kiss her lips. "It is so good to see you again," she said in excellent English. "And you must be my American counterpart, Megan O'Riley," she said pleasantly, turning to Megan, who was trying not to feel like a disgruntled wife at the sight of Case kissing the Frenchwoman on the lips.

"You must be Cecile," Megan replied with excessive politeness. "I'm very glad to meet you."

Cecile's eyebrows drifted upward in a quizzical expression for a fleeting moment, and then she was drawing Megan and Case forward and introducing the others.

"Case, you already know Marcelle and Yvette."

At this point Cecile broke into rapid French. Megan caught her own name and smiled in acknowledgement of the introduction, her eyes lingering on the model whom she had seen in photographs in magazines. Megan would have recognized Marcelle but she looked considerably different in person, no older than her twenty-one years but harder somehow. A mere inch under six feet, she was thin to the point of gauntness, her black hair coarse-textured and sleeked straight back from her face, her eyes like huge black coals and made to look even larger by makeup Megan found almost macabre.

The outfit Marcelle wore was one of the designer fashions she would model in the magazine feature, but in this real-life, casual setting, the dramatic evening ensemble was patently absurd. The metallic gold miniskirt glittered with silver and gold beading. A matching overblouse had enormous wing sleeves. The model's long legs looked even longer than they were in white kid boots laced up to the thigh with gold thongs. With no jewelry except gold bracelets, and she had at least a dozen of these on one arm from wrist to elbow, Marcelle looked like some exotic, larger-than-life species of the human race.

In striking contrast was the young woman introduced as Yvette. Slender and quietly attractive, with dark hair and eyes, she had "class" etched in her manner and dress. The few words she spoke in response to Cecile's introduction of Megan revealed that her voice was as cultured as her appearance was indicative of breeding. She definitely wasn't Megan's preconceived notion of the famous model's personal attendant.

Nor was the nondescript young man introduced as René what Megan had expected in a French hairstylist and makeup expert of some reputation. Polite and distant, he wasn't strikingly masculine but neither was he affected and effeminate in his speech and mannerisms. He was distressingly ordinary.

It was difficult for Megan not to be disappointed in the whole lot of them. Not a single one of them quite lived up to her expectations. Marcelle didn't strike the weakest chord of envy inside Megan's breast. If anything, Megan sensed something almost forlorn about the young model in the ridiculous costume and felt a pang akin to sympathy. Marcelle seldom spoke, usually seeking out Yvette's gaze beforehand as though somehow asking her approval, and her voice came as a shock to Megan. Low and husky, it had a rough, uncultivated timbre that grated on the nerves and hinted at a low-class background.

The conversation was a rapid mixture of French and English, with Cecile translating for the benefit of Case and Megan and with Yvette doing most of the talking for Marcelle. After the most perfunctory attention to the social amenities, the talk centered on their reason for being there, the magazine feature.

Megan quickly lost her initial fascination in studying the people with whom she would be working and let her gaze drift around the crowded bar, listening to her companions with only one ear. There were guests from the hotel, the women dressed in colorful long skirts and dresses, the men in slacks and shirts but, for the most part, not wearing jackets and ties. Somehow it was easy for her to pick out the yachtsmen from the anchored sailboats, not so much from any distinctive difference in dress but from subtle differences of manner. There was a weathered toughness, an air of confidence about the men and a quiet competence in the women that in no way negated their femininity.

Shifting her gaze outward toward the water, Megan sighed softly, entranced with what she saw. The anchor lights on the yachts were like fireflies in the darkness. Larger and glowing more steadily were the lights of the several restaurants on the opposite shore. These seemed to beckon and promise romance. Megan found herself wishing she and Case were alone tonight, not with Cecile and Yvette, so intent upon all the details of doing the feature, nor with Marcelle and René, who though participating little in the discussion apparently felt none of Megan's impatience with it.

Wouldn't it be perfectly marvelous, Megan thought wistfully, to be all alone with Case in this foreign, exotic setting, sipping cool rum drinks and talking, not arguing. After a while they could walk along the beach near the water, gaze up at a sky she visualized as inky black and studded with stars— pure conjecture on her part, since it hadn't been fully dark when they arrived. The thatched roof over her head kept her from testing out her hypothesis.

It was an enormous effort for Megan to drag her wandering thoughts back to the present the way it really was rather than the way she would have liked it to have been. Turning back toward her party, she worked at looking interested. Unexpectedly, Case caught her eye and winked, letting her know he had been keeping track of her the entire time.

"The others are about to order another round of planter's punches," he told her. "After the drinks we had with Jacques and Alina and now this one, I could use some fresh air to clear my head. What about you?"

Megan was almost discomfitted for a moment, wondering if Case had read her mind. Then she eagerly confirmed that she would love to go for a walk, meanwhile admonishing herself not to give a romantic interpretation to his desire to get away from the others. It was highly doubtful that Case intended to make any intimate overtures.

Megan found herself unable to take the sound advice of her common sense. Her body was alive tonight and filled with those woman's needs she had suppressed for two years out of necessity, living apart from her husband. The thought of being in Case's arms again, of having him kiss her and caress her body, brought on such longing that her breathing was shallow, shortchanging her lungs of the oxygen it needed.

As they left the others Case took her arm and led her along a paved walkway illuminated enough for safety but not enough to dispel the magic of the tropical evening. Down near the sand beach, they skirted a thatched-roof building perched half on the grass and half on the sand and found themselves in a quieter world, far enough away from the bar so that the human voices and laughter were subdued and distant.

The sky was as magnificent as Megan had imagined it to be, huge and black and pricked with millions of diamond stars. The scent of blossoms on the night air went straight to her head, an elixir that intoxicated. From out on the water came the faint hollow tapping of metal on metal as the breeze caught a slack piece of stainless steel wire and slapped it against a mast. Over on the St. Vincent side of the water there was the startlingly clear sound of voices, a man's and then a woman's followed by the woman's laughter.

Megan expelled a deep sigh.

"Oh, Case! Isn't this wonderful!" she exulted softly.

Case was still holding her arm. He dropped it now and paced away from her several steps, his hands pushed down deep into his pockets.

"Those rum punches go down easy, too easy," was his disappointing reply. "The last thing I want is to start a job like this one with a hangover."

The job, the job—forget the damned job! Megan felt like blurting out. Choking back the words, she reminded herself once again of the facts. She was a professional, here to do a job. If she expected Case to take her career aspirations seriously, she had to remember that.

Case braced himself as Megan came closer and stopped. It took every ounce of his self-control not to take her in his arms. He didn't dare. There was the rest of this evening to get through. And besides, he didn't know how she would react. If she repulsed him, he really didn't know what he would do. Then there was that deeper, darker fear that warned him he shouldn't start anything he might not be able to finish.

Megan draped the cardigan around her shoulders and took a deep breath to steady her emotions.

"Now that I've had a chance to meet the others and make my own impressions, would you mind filling me in a little on your opinions?" she asked almost timidly. The strange quality of the silence that met this request made her wonder what was going on in Case's thoughts. Had she read the situation accurately? He did want everything between them businesslike, didn't he?

"Marcelle isn't at all what I expected," Megan went on nervously. "She isn't even really pretty, is she? And she seems almost unsure of herself." Megan didn't add the rest of what she was thinking. She would never have believed Case if he came home from an assignment like this one and told her he didn't find the model attractive. She'd always had her own ideas of what his work must be like, and she'd never really taken seriously any remarks of his that conflicted with her own preconceived notions.

Case kicked at the sand with the toe of one leather moccasin.

"She's a poor kid from the wrong side of the tracks who happens to have superb bone structure and photographs well. I don't know the whole story, but she owes her career and success to Yvette, who tells her how many steps to take in any one direction and when to take them."

"I got the impression that Marcelle is dependent on Yvette just in the few minutes I was around them," Megan said reflectively. "And it's so obvious

that Yvette *is* from the right side of the tracks."
Megan was privately pleased with the confidentiality
of their exchange.

"As you'd expect, there are rumors about the
relationship," Case was continuing, obviously not
approving of the gossip. "All I know for sure—and
all I really care about, for that matter—is that Yvette
does a damned good job as Marcelle's manager and
agent. The girl wouldn't stand a chance on her
own."

Megan had to agree with that last. She pictured
Marcelle in the outlandish costume back in the bar
and felt again that twinge of sympathy for the young
woman she barely knew.

"What about Cecile? What do you think of her?"
Megan told herself there was nothing personal in the
inquiry. She was merely curious to see if her own
impressions matched Case's in regard to the French
writer.

"She's good at her job and not a bad sort," Case
replied readily. "Hard as nails," he added matter-of-
factly.

Megan felt herself go on the defensive.

"I don't know—I kind of liked her," she countered quickly, as though Case had offered some
unfair criticism when actually he had not. "I was
kind of expecting her to be antagonistic toward me,
but she didn't seem that way at all."

Case shrugged.

"Cecile's tops in her field in France. You're really
no threat to her as a relatively unknown American
writer."

Megan winced a little under the bluntness but couldn't argue with the all-too-obvious explanation.

"I guess you're right," she admitted ruefully, realizing suddenly why she had tried to defend Cecile and only exposed herself in the process. Cecile had already attained the professional recognition Megan herself would like to have. It had rankled that Case wasn't more admiring of Cecile as a woman, even though he readily conceded her competency in her work.

"Ready to go back and join the others?"

Case's inquiry broke into her thoughts. Instinctively she wished that she could delay the inevitable and keep him there a while longer, all to herself, but he was continuing in a voice that indicated his thoughts had already returned to the business at hand, the magazine feature.

"They should be ready for dinner by now. I want to eat and get back to the boat early. We can all do with a good night's sleep before we start tomorrow."

Megan didn't answer as reluctantly she fell into step beside him, battling a sense of letdown. The evening had promised so much and was turning out to be a disappointment in a way she could hardly explain to Case. Once again she reminded herself of her professional priorities and determined to concentrate on business throughout the remainder of the evening, just as the others were doing.

Throughout dinner she listened carefully and joined in from time to time in the discussion that once again centered on the magazine feature. With one part of her mind she noted that Case's opinion carried great weight with both Cecile and Yvette. They made no effort to conceal their respect for his work and their pleasure that he was working with them on the assignment. Megan felt a great sense of pride and a possessiveness she had to work at not revealing.

When the meal was over, Case announced at once his intention of returning to *l'Esprit* before anyone could even suggest stopping at the bar for a nightcap. The tender from the schooner was on hand to take him and Megan and the others to their respective vessels.

Megan was gripped by a strange mixture of apprehension and anticipation as she boarded the yacht that would be her floating hotel for the next two weeks. Jacques and Alina had not returned from their dinner ashore. The *l'Esprit* dinghy was nowhere in sight. Megan and Case were alone together for the first time in two years. Every nerve in her body seemed ignited with the awareness of that fact, and she knew, as Case stepped down into the cockpit with her, that he felt the electricity in the air between them. Megan's heartbeat accelerated to a dizzying rate of speed as a tense silence stretched out. She could not read his intentions and thus had no inkling as to what her next move should be. It was an excruciating moment with herself balanced precariously between not wanting to make a wrong assumption and risk her pride and yet not wanting to discourage him from an overture that would lead to intimacy.

"It's a good thing Jacques remembered to give you a key," she said finally, her voice a half note too high and the words falling out too rapidly, hinting at her nervousness.

Case began digging in his pocket at once, as though her observation had served as a reminder.

"Yes. A good thing," he said almost distractedly.

Megan waited in a frenzy of uncertainty while he finally pulled out the key and set about unlocking the padlock on the hatch. What was Case thinking and feeling this moment? she wondered desperately. Did he want to make love to her? Did he want to sleep with her in the same bed and hold her the way he once had done? Did he have any idea at all how much she wanted both of those things, wanted them so badly she ached?

Case deliberately fumbled with the lock, stalling for time. Megan had been as nervous as a cat ever since they left Young Island and headed back for the yacht, and then when she saw the dinghy missing and realized Jacques and Alina weren't aboard, she'd started sending out panic signals he couldn't fail to decipher. She was afraid he would try to make love to her. Didn't she want him anymore? Was there somebody else? Jealousy stabbed his guts at the thought of another man making love to her. As the key fitted into the padlock, Case knew suddenly he had to have more time. He wasn't ready yet to deal with the truth, whatever it was.

"How about a nightcap?" he suggested at the same time that he slid the hatch cover back. Inwardly he had to marvel at the tone he had been able to produce, light and casual as though he and a stranger he had just met were about to part outside their separate hotel doors.

Megan blinked in confusion for several seconds and then experienced a surge of angry resentment. There she had stood in an agony of uncertainty, wondering if Case wanted to go to bed with her, and all he had on his mind was a drink!

"Sure—why not?" Megan replied grimly, plopping down on a cockpit cushion and telling herself how glad she was she hadn't said or done anything to let Case know what *she* had been thinking. She might die of sexual frustration on this trip, but Case would never suspect how much she wanted him to make love to her.

Case sensed the swift change in Megan's mood, and while not fully comprehending it, he could tell the nervousness had gone. As relieved as he was let down, he went down into the boat to mix the drinks, taking his time about it.

"What is it?" Megan asked in a slightly disgruntled tone when Case came up and handed her a glass.

"Rum, fresh lime juice, and water," he answered, settling down on the cockpit seat opposite her. "What do you think of it?"

Something conciliatory in his voice and manner arrested her attention and threatened to disarm her. Megan held fast to her sense of injury as she raised the glass to her lips and took a sip.

"It's refreshing," she conceded.

After that neither of them said anything for a while. Megan began to wish she had been more receptive to his efforts toward truce. It was probably silly of her to feel she had been rejected just on the basis of her own perception.

"Well, now that you've put in your first day on a foreign assignment, what do you think?" Case asked finally, stretching out full length on the long cushion with a deep sigh of relaxation. "Does it all measure up to your expectations?"

Megan could detect nothing other than interest in the inquiry. She thought for a moment, wanting to be truthful without revealing too much. After what had just happened—or *hadn't* happened—Case wasn't to know how much she had expected from this trip personally, as well as professionally.

"I'm not exactly disappointed," she began reflectively, "but there have been some surprises. For one thing, the people we're working with aren't at all what I expected. They seem so . . . so *ordinary*. I mean, just like regular people. Even Marcelle, in spite of the way she looks. When I think of the photographs I've seen of her and then compare that to the way she is in person . . ." Megan struggled to pinpoint the difference she perceived and sought to express.

Case picked his glass up from where he had set it in the cockpit well between the seats and raised up enough to take a sip. He sounded oddly pleased when he spoke.

"The person you saw in the photographs *isn't* Marcelle, the real human being. She's an illusion. People like Cecile and myself take the real Marcelle and use her as 'raw material' to create a mirage to satisfy some strange craving women have for make-believe glamour." He was silent a moment, considering his own observations. "I guess I shouldn't sound so critical or even waste my time trying to understand it. After all, I've cashed in on it for a number of years.''

Megan found the edge of self-derision in his voice profoundly disturbing. She wished she could ignore it as though it hadn't been there.

"You're not sorry you went into fashion photography, are you, Case?" she asked reluctantly, dreading his answer. They both knew why he had gone into the field—to make money to support his new wife and unborn child.

Case wasn't oblivious to the way she had phrased the question. He knew the answer she would have liked to hear, but he couldn't in honesty give it to her. Still, he had no desire to make her feel guilt for decisions he had made entirely on his own for good reason. He would do it all again if he had to.

"I'm not 'sorry,'" he replied reasonably. "I needed to make a living for a family, and I hoped I could manage to do that with a camera. My work has allowed me to do both of those things. And technically speaking, fashion photography has been challenging. It's hard to keep coming up with an approach that's fresh." He made a derogatory sound. "I'd be lying if I said the recognition isn't flattering, not to mention that I get paid extraordinarily well. But it's not the kind of work I'd want to do the rest of my life."

Megan was silent as she tried to assimilate that last statement and decide if it really surprised her. Hadn't Case been telling her his feelings indirectly for years? Somehow she'd never taken his remarks seriously, unable to believe that any man could *not* like what he did for a living: photograph beautiful women. She yearned to question him about the kind of work he would like to get into, but the situation was an extremely delicate one. She didn't want him to think her interest was purely mercenary and that she was worried he might not continue to provide a high standard of living for herself and the children as he currently did on his substantial income.

For the past two years while he and Megan were separated, Case had continued to pay all the running family expenses just as though he were still living at home. The only difference was that Megan used none of the money in their joint checking account for her personal expenses. She bought her clothes and makeup and paid for her commuting expenses out of her own salary.

Megan worked with enough women who were separated from their husbands or divorced to know her situation was anything but common. When she thought about it at all, she felt vaguely guilty for accepting Case's generosity under the circumstances, and yet she didn't think it was fair for the children to be deprived of what their father was well able to give them.

"Worrying about the kids again?"

Megan came back to the present, realizing she had taken a deep breath and expelled it in a troubled sigh. For a moment she considered refuting Case's interpretation of her moody introspection, but then it occurred to her he may have offered it as a change of subject. In a way she *was* thinking about the children.

"I've never been this far away from them," she said, suddenly feeling wistful. "It'll probably do them good." When Case didn't reply, she cast around for something light and cheerful to say. Remembering a recent conversation with her twelve-year-old daughter, Megan chuckled aloud. "By the way, do you know Kathleen's biggest worry these days? She's the only one in her little group of girlfriends who hasn't begun to develop breasts. I happened upon her poring over all the old family photo albums. She was checking the pictures of her female ancestors on both sides of the family at the age of twelve!"

Megan could see the white gleam of Case's smile in the semidarkness, some faint illumination being provided by the anchor light and the moon. He was amused as she had intended him to be.

"Kathleen had better keep her fingers crossed that she takes after her mother in that respect and not after the Ballentine women," he joked lightly.

There was nothing overtly complimentary about the comment to make Megan feel so inordinately pleased nor to cause the sudden tingling awareness of her firmly rounded breasts, which had already budded into prominence by the time she was Kathleen's age.

"I'm afraid you and I may have messed things up a bit when we were distributing the genes to our kids," she suggested laughingly. "Kathleen got your height while poor Danny seems doomed to be a peewee like his mother. He worries constantly that he won't grow tall enough to play basketball in high school, which—as you know—is his greatest ambition."

Megan heard the flirtatious undertone in her voice and held her breath for his response. To her disappointment and deepening puzzlement, his mood suddenly underwent a drastic change. Apparently no longer amused with the trivial worries of their children, he seemed deeply buried in thought, miles away from Megan, who frantically searched her recent joking remarks for some clue to what might have caused him to withdraw. She was about to gather her courage and ask him point-blank what was wrong when he stirred restlessly and sat up. Reaching down for his glass, he took a sip and tossed the remainder of the contents over the side, having consumed almost none of the drink he had seemed to want a few minutes ago.

"Case, I'm sorry if I said something . . ." Megan began hesitantly. In the distance she could hear the sudden sound of an outboard coming to life and wondered if Jacques and Alina were returning.

"You didn't say anything wrong," Case dismissed impatiently. "It's just that sometimes I realize how much I'm missing not being around the kids. And they're growing up so damned fast—"

Case broke off, looking away into the darkness toward the sound of the outboard, which was growing steadily louder. He hadn't been totally honest with Megan just now. How could he tell her he had heard the subtle invitation in her voice and wanted more than anything in the world to cross the space between them in the cockpit, to take her into his arms, to feel in his hands again the warm, straining curves of her breasts—but that he was afraid? No, he couldn't risk telling her, and in all probability Jacques and Alina were on their way to the boat and would be here any second.

Feeling like a split personality, Case willed the approaching dinghy to go on by to another of the anchored boats and yet at the same time he prayed for the imminent arrival of the French couple. It might be silly, but he felt as though he were hanging in the balance of fate. If Jacques and Alina came aboard in a few seconds, Case would excuse himself as soon as possible and go to bed, despising himself for putting off the inevitable and yet relieved not to know the worst. If they *didn't* come back soon . . .

Megan bit down hard on her bottom lip, deliberately hurting herself and swallowing hard at the big lump in her throat. What could she say to Case except "I'm sorry," and that sounded pitifully inadequate in the face of his emotion. She felt like a criminal and yet her reason told her it wasn't all *her* fault Case had moved out of the house and was missing so much of his children's growing up years. He was the one who had issued an unreasonable ultimatum and split up their family, wasn't he? Or was Megan to blame for holding fast to her insistence that she could be a wife and mother and still have a career?

Torn once again by an inner debate no less agonizing for all its dreary familiarity, Megan found it difficult to be sociable when Jacques and Alina came aboard and joined Megan and Case in the cockpit. For all the sense of anticlimax, she was relieved when Case made the first move and announced his intention of going to bed. Taking his cue, they all went down below to their separate staterooms for the night.

As she undressed and climbed into her double

bunk, Megan was no closer to assigning blame for the problems separating Case and herself. Wearily she shoved the whole complicated situation out of her mind. Tomorrow was another day. It was disappointing that she and Case had brought along with them these insoluble conflicts to a place so beautiful, so perfect that everyone should be happy here. Silly romantic that she was, Megan had hoped this trip would have the curative effect of a second honeymoon. Alone in her bunk, disconcerted by the unfamiliar movements of the boat and the noises of the night, she felt anything but optimistic about the future.

Chapter Five

The next day was long and grueling and yet utterly fascinating for Megan, who got a first glimpse of how much toil could go into a glossy magazine feature depicting life as idyllic and leisurely. It was a revelation for her to see Case at work. He was tireless, a relentless taskmaster who drove everyone else as hard as he pushed himself. Using every technique in the book to get what he wanted from Marcelle, he would flatter, cajole, scold, or—if all else failed—subject her to such biting sarcasm that Megan had to hold back words of protest, reminding herself she had no right to reprimand Case. She was there as a writer, not as his wife.

The entire day's photographing was done on Young Island, the whole of which belonged to the Young Island hotel. The steep, cobblestone paths provided innumerable picturesque settings for Marcelle, who was wearing vivid summer costumes that rivaled the brilliant blossoms. Several lookouts afforded views that took Megan's breath away and made her wish she were enjoying all this as it should be enjoyed. The same kind of wistfulness struck her when Case was photographing Marcelle on the beach in a smart maillot that was the very latest in designer beachwear. With sweat trickling underneath Megan's sticky cotton top and culottes, she thought longingly of being in a swimsuit herself and plunging into that cool, inviting water that lapped against the shore.

That afternoon when she returned to the yacht with Case, the others having gone back to the schooner, Megan found herself more than willing to take the rest Case had recommended for all of them. After a cool shower, she felt strangely exhausted and fell asleep almost at once when she lay down on her bunk. Awakening an hour and a half later, she remembered what Case had said on the flight down: that it was difficult to take advantage of spare time with sightseeing because one frequently didn't have the energy. Now she wasn't quite so certain he was wrong.

Early in the evening, work was resumed at the Young Island bar, where Case photographed Marcelle in the same evening costume she had worn the previous night. The hotel guests good-naturedly cooperated, sitting or standing wherever Case directed them.

"That's it," he announced finally and set about at once packing up his gear with the help of two young deckhands from the schooner, who had assisted him with setting up and moving lights that they would now take back to the schooner for safe storage.

"Case, you're as much a slave driver as I remembered," Cecile accused, coming up to him, a drink in her hand. "You two want to stay here and have a drink with us before we go on back to the schooner for dinner?"

"Not me," Case refused from his crouching position where he was packing cameras and lenses into a leather case. He hadn't even glanced up at Megan to gauge her feelings. "And count me out for dinner on the schooner, too," he added.

Cecile didn't look surprised.

"Still antisocial the way I remembered, too," she said without any real resentment and turned away to join the others at the bar, obviously assuming that Megan would do whatever Case opted to do.

Megan felt a stir of irritation that she hadn't been consulted by either of them.

"I wasn't aware that we were invited to eat dinner with Jacques and Alina on the boat," she observed with an edge to her tone that drew a close look from Case as he rose and slipped the strap of the leather case over one shoulder.

"We aren't," he confirmed. "I'm sure they wouldn't mind if we gave them some advance notice, but it's not a part of the deal for them to feed us meals except when we're under way, moving from one anchorage to another. I thought I'd try one of those places over there tonight." He nodded his head over toward the St. Vincent shoreline, some six hundred yards away. Realizing how flat he had sounded, he added, "I've had enough make-believe glamour for one day. The last thing I want to do is spend the evening talking shop."

After he had taken a step, Case realized Megan wasn't falling into step beside him. Turning, he looked back at her inquiringly.

"Coming with me?"

As far as Megan was concerned, it was the first hint of invitation and not a very warm one at that.

"Are you sure you want me?"

Case was clearly taken aback at the unmistakable uncertainty side by side with the defensiveness in her tone. He frowned at himself for having been too brusque and for having taken too much for granted, mainly that she would know he welcomed her presence, no matter what.

"Of course I 'want' you."

His inflection had an immediate and regenerative effect upon both of them. Case could feel the swift flow of adrenalin to his tired mind and body. Megan's drooping spirits suddenly took wing and she looked forward to the evening ahead with the keenest anticipation.

Seeing the sparkle in her vivid blue eyes, Case remembered what the trip meant to her. He looked back at the bar, trying to see it the way Megan might, a glamorous set in a movie depicting the tropical fun of the Caribbean, for those who could afford it.

"Don't feel like you have to stick with me if you'd rather stay here with the others," he said hesitantly, obviously not thrilled with the notion of leaving her behind.

"I'd rather go with you," Megan answered promptly, slipping her hand under his arm. She didn't want to spend the evening talking shop either. Last night as she stood with the others in the Young Island bar, she had fantasized about having Case alone to herself. He was offering her the reality.

Jacques lent them the dinghy for the evening, since he and Alina would not be needing it. They were entertaining cruising acquaintances who had just arrived at the anchorage in their sailboat that afternoon.

"Your chariot awaits, ma'am," Case teased as he held the small boat securely to the side of the yacht while Megan climbed down the ladder, her sandals in one hand.

"I see why people finally give up on shoes and just go barefoot," she observed happily, proud of herself that already she felt quite agile and confident in this new habitat where one got about in dinghies and launches.

"I'm just glad you gals don't give up skirts," Case countered suggestively, making Megan aware that she was giving him a view of slim bare legs and undoubtedly a provocative glimpse of her black lace bikini panties, too, as she descended the ladder, wearing a black-and-white print sundress.

Her smile was frankly flirtatious as she settled herself in the seat facing him as he sat at the stern. She felt young and flighty like a teenage girl on a date with a handsome guy, not like a wife and mother with the man she'd been married to for more than a decade. And Case was without any doubt very handsome tonight in natural muslin trousers, the kind with a drawstring waist—popular she'd noticed with the cruising yachtsmen—and a dark blue shirt. Already looking tanned from a day in the tropics, he might have been a captain off of one of the yachts in the anchorage. There was a rakish slant to his smile, a gleam in his dark eyes that made her remember the way he had been when she first met him, an impulsive, happy-go-lucky young man of twenty-four who never went anywhere without his camera and managed to sell enough of the pictures he took to make a meager living.

"This is such *fun!*" she exulted as he started the outboard and sent the small boat skimming over the water to the same dock near which they had been deposited upon their arrival in St. Vincent.

They ate dinner at one of the several restaurants, deciding upon the Pink Dolphin, whose proprietor was an Englishman. Located in a wooden frame building whose plain facade matched the lack of pretension in the inside decor as well as the menu, the restaurant nonetheless offered the delight of an open dining gallery overlooking the water. The night was fragrant with the scent of blossoms borne on the breeze. Across the channel Young Island was a tiny land of enchantment with lanterns gleaming along its steep hillsides.

Megan couldn't have cared less what she ate, but when their food was served, she discovered she was very hungry and ate with appetite. When they had finished their meal and were waiting for coffee, a group of six people trooped in, chatting volubly in a foreign tongue as they seated themselves with a certain amount of flurry. Megan watched with open interest, thinking privately that two of the men looked like gnomes.

"I don't know—German maybe, or Swedish," Case suggested in reply to the inquiry she had made simply by looking at him with raised brows.

Megan heaved a happy little sigh and decided she would burst if she didn't express the way she felt.

"Oh, Case—I'm so *glad* I'm here. At this moment the world seems so big and various and . . . and *exciting!*" Her lips curved into an irrepressible smile to compensate for the inadequacy of words. Her eyes implored him not to deride her naive enthusiasm.

His response took her utterly by surprise since she had been expecting a teasing remark. Case was a man of deep feelings but not of flowery words.

"I'm glad you're here, too," he said with simple gravity and picked up her hand, which was lying on the table between them. He pressed it to his lips and held it there for a long wonderful moment.

Megan felt her heart swell with painful joy at the incredible rightness of the words and the gesture and the deep sincerity of his emotion. There were a thousand things she wanted to say all at once. A thousand questions she wished she could ask. Somehow it all had to do with the lost opportunities in the past and the possibilities of making up for them in the future. But her woman's instincts bade her to be quiet, to savor the sweetness and implicit eloquence of the present. The past held too much bitterness and the future was far too tenuous. To Megan's own inner amazement, she was able to do what she had done seldom in her lifetime: hold her tongue.

After dinner they went into the adjoining bar, a long narrow room with booths along the outside wall and a door that stood open. There were stools along the high counter opposite the booths. The wood floor was bare, without paint or varnish.

Most of the patrons of the bar had the distinct mark of cruising sailors, the men deeply tanned and most of them bearded, the women equally as tanned and wearing cool, comfortable clothing that bared much of their smooth skin to view.

Megan felt amazingly as though she had walked into the midst of a party to which she had been invited without knowing either the hosts or the guests. She and Case were greeted at once by a tall, red-haired man who called Case "mate" and spoke in a rolling Australian accent. Everyone in the bar stopped and listened while Case introduced himself and Megan and explained they were part of the magazine crew on the *Marie Antoinette* and *l'Esprit*. Their connection with the cruising assembly seemed thereby established.

Megan found herself chatting with first one person and then another, men and women, from countries all over the world, most of whom spoke English remarkably well and yet seemed not to expect her to speak any language but her own once it was established she was American. Before long she was pressed into taking her turn in the dart game competition, which was going on just outside the open door where the dart board hung on the clapboard siding.

Afterward she stood and watched Case while he played, listening to the rich spontaneity of his deep laugh and his quick contributions to the ceaseless repartee spoken in a half-dozen different accents. A few hours earlier Cecile had called him antisocial, but he looked anything but that now. He was completely at ease in a situation lacking the artificial glamour he had come to the tropics to capture—or more aptly to create—with his camera. Megan had come with him on this assignment hungry for that glamour, and yet this evening had a magic all its own that she would always treasure.

It was more than the novelty of meeting so many interesting people from backgrounds different from her own. Tonight she felt as though she had gotten back on track with Case. They were together even when he stood at one end of the room and she at the other. She was intensely aware of his presence every second, and the awareness only heightened her other perceptions and her enjoyment of her companions. It didn't isolate her.

She would look around in the middle of a conversation and catch his eye on her. They would smile at each other to confirm what was oddly thrilling under the circumstances: the mere fact that they were there *together*. When they were standing close to each other, they touched again with all that old ease and naturalness of their comfortable married years, and yet something new was added. The familiar was infused with an altogether pleasurable strangeness that vibrated through all the cells in Megan's body and made her intensely aware of her sexuality, aware of Case's virility. The attraction between them was like a minor theme in the background, heightening their participation in the moment and then growing steadily stronger until it was no longer a minor theme but what the evening was really all about.

As the hour grew later, Megan found herself becoming restive. It grew more and more difficult to carry on conversation with jovial strangers, no matter how interesting they might be or how fascinating their backgrounds. She was waiting for a signal from Case that it was time to go, an acknowledgement of the urgency that had been steadily building inside her.

When he was suddenly beside her near one end of the long high counter, she turned toward him and smiled the question in her mind: *Are you ready to go?*

"How about one more drink?" he asked quickly.

Megan felt a pang of disappointment that put a tiny rift in the perfect accord she had reveled in all evening. Why did Case want to stay here instead of being alone with her? That question brought a tremor of uncertainty to the pit of her stomach. It occurred to her suddenly that Case had been drinking more tonight than was his habit. She decided to use that as the basis of her refusal.

"I think we've both had enough to drink," she refused a little too primly. "Tomorrow's another working day, remember."

Case felt a little jolt down inside his gut that said

he couldn't put off the inevitable any longer. They couldn't stay here in the bar all night. Megan was right—tomorrow was another working day, and would probably be worse than today had been. God, he wished now he hadn't had so much to drink. He had just needed to unwind—Oh, hell, what was the use of making excuses.

"You're right," he agreed quietly. "We'd better go."

The tense awareness between them was almost palpable as they left the Pink Dolphin and entered the fragrant darkness of the night, walking the short distance along a rutted dirt street and turning left toward the pier, where they had left the dinghy. Megan wished desperately that she could do or say something to ease Case's sudden constraint. He had been touching her casually all evening in the bar, laying an arm across her shoulders, coming up behind her and curving his hands around the narrowness of her waist. Now he didn't even take her hand.

Why is he so awkward now that we're alone? She could think of only two reasons. If he was unsure of whether she would welcome intimacy, she could certainly handle that. But the alternative explanation struck terror in her heart and put an edge of fear on the anticipation that had been building inside her all evening. *What if he didn't want to make love to her anymore?*

"Case, I've had such a wonderful time tonight," she told him softly, the imploring tone in her voice adding what had been left unsaid: *Please touch me.* Perhaps he didn't know how much she longed to have him hold her and make love to her as he always had.

Case cleared his throat.

"Watch your step," he advised gruffly and took her arm with a jerky motion as they came to the edge of the pier. Unexpectedly she stopped and turned straight into him. Case felt the impact of her body against his and groaned aloud. Beyond thinking now and beyond fearing consequences, he gathered her up close against him, feeling her warmness and the wonderful softness of her woman's curves.

"Ah, Meg, you *feel* so damned *good,*" he muttered before his mouth found hers and claimed the willing softness he remembered so well. The hunger inside him swelled like a great balloon and then sharpened into an ache he feared he would never be able to assuage. Control slipped away as his mouth devoured hers with an insatiable need and his tongue pushed into her mouth and found hers, arched and hot and sweetly urgent.

Even as he held her tight against him and kissed her with all the pent up hunger of two years of deprivation, Case fought against the panic that gripped him as he realized he wanted her too much. Her arms were tight around his neck, her breasts straining into his chest, her mouth moving and eager on his. All these signals of her willingness to have him make love to her registered in his brain and wreaked havoc with his already rampant senses.

Feeling the great shudders ripping through his body, hearing his breathing as it came in gusts, Case knew he was like a starving man faced with a too-sumptuous feast. He wanted to grab everything at once with his trembling hands and stuff the too-rich food into his mouth in a frenzy even while his stomach quaked and his brain urged caution. He *had* to calm down a little.

Megan felt herself taken by storm and let her own passion rise up to meet the urgency of Case's. She sensed an element of desperation as he tore his mouth away from the clinging eagerness of hers and murmured her name over and over as he buried his face into the curve of her neck. His hot breath against her skin brought shivers of pleasure.

She had every intention of saying something to reassure him that everything was all right, but at that moment he lifted the skirt of her sundress and she moaned his name aloud instead, forgetting everything but her own trembling eagerness as his hands slipped inside the elastic waist of her panties and caressed the firm curves of her buttocks. Not satisfied, they slid upward over her hips and then back down, pushing the flimsy nylon and lace garment down around her thighs. Finally came the intimacy Megan had been waiting for as one hand curved over the soft swell between her legs, pressing and kneading and then probing with a bold finger to discover the telltale wetness.

"Case!" Megan gasped his name aloud, making of it a plea as much as an admission. As he stroked, his fingers seemed to be directly touching and inflaming the ache throbbing insistently between her legs.

"We can't stay here," she said desperately, doing nothing to bring the situation under control as she slid her hands from around his neck and caressed the broad expanse of his chest, loving the solidness and the strength. "Oh, Case, I want you to make love to me *so* much!" she murmured in a voice softened with her passion. Her hands were exploring downward now and finding the hard, swollen proof that he wanted her as much as she wanted him. "It's been so long. *Too* long. We never disappointed each other in bed, did we? Whatever other problems we might have had . . ."

The change in his body was instant, bringing confusion to Megan's dazed mind. He recoiled and then seemed to resist the intimate massaging of her hand. Before she knew what was happening, he had taken his hands away from her and stepped back.

"You're right," he said in a strangled voice that brought a faint chill along her flesh. "This is hardly the place."

Megan knew that something had suddenly gone terribly wrong, but she didn't know what. It was patently obvious she hadn't been resisting him. He couldn't be feeling that he had been rebuffed. And what had there been in her words to upset him? She had only been voicing her honest feelings that whatever their marital problems, their sex life had always been fantastic. Her blood suddenly ran cold as she considered an explanation she didn't know if she could bear: Had she been blind in thinking their lovemaking was as totally satisfactory for him as it had been for her? During the two years of their separation, had Case discovered more pleasure in the arms of other women than in hers?

Megan quickly brushed aside the absurd fear, reminding herself that Case had been fully aroused just now. That was hardly something a man could

fake. Probably nothing was wrong. It had undoubtedly been difficult for him to control his passion just
as it had been anything but easy for her to stop. In
the privacy of one of their cabins, they could take up
where they left off.

"I hope Jacques and Alina have already gone to
bed," she ventured as they walked along the pier to
the place where the dinghy was tied. Case didn't
reply as he pulled the dinghy up close and stepped
down into it. Megan's confidence wavered as she got
down into the dinghy, too, and took her place,
feeling much more clumsy now than she had a few
hours earlier. Case started the outboard with a
vicious pull that hinted of violence, and the sound of
the motor filled the night quiet. Megan was grateful
for the darkness and oblivious to the charms of the
evening she had found so tantalizing to the senses on
the ride to the pier.

She climbed aboard first and waited in the cockpit
for Case, who came aboard, too, and led the dinghy
aft, fastening the painter to a cleat. When he stepped
down into the cockpit and stood there several feet
away from her, she swallowed to try to rid her throat
of its dryness. Anxiously she waited for him to say
something to dispel her uncertainty and the sense
that something was wrong.

"God, I'm bushed."

The weariness in the deep sigh was real, but Case
knew Meg had probably caught the strain in his
voice. He heard her catch her breath and could sense
her stiffening.

As she climbed down the companionway ladder

ahead of Case, Megan battled with herself. No, she would *not* ask him point-blank what was wrong. If he wanted to pretend nothing had happened between them over there on the pier, she would do the same.

But then in the passageway separating their two cabins, he took both her shoulders in his big, gentle hands and pressed a light kiss to her lips.

"Good night," he said huskily in a low voice that brought to the surface all her tightly clamped emotions and smashed her resolution to hold to her pride. "Sleep well, honey."

The sadness and the regret in his tone brought a sting of tears to Megan's eyes, and she blinked hard.

"How can I—sleep well?" she demanded, her voice cracking with hurt and indignation. Swallowing, she continued with difficulty. "What's wrong, Case? Don't you want to make love to me anymore? We're still married, and even if we weren't, we're both adults. Is it because we're separated, and you're still angry with me?"

Case tensed all his muscles, closing his eyes a brief second as he summoned all his reserves of judgment and restraint. God, he was tempted to take her into his arms and blurt out his guts, hoping for the best. But he just *couldn't* take the chance. Too damned much was at stake, and the truth was he just wasn't sure of her now after two years. If he tried to make love to her, dead tired and a little drunk, it might not be good for her, the way she remembered. No, better to wait. Better to be as sure as possible.

Steeling his determination, Case opened his eyes and told her as much of the truth as he dared.

"I'm just tired, honey," he said apologetically. "That's all. Honest. And I drank a little too much tonight."

Megan wasn't convinced. He hadn't been too tired or too drunk a few minutes ago to kiss her and caress her body into a fever pitch of desire. It was hardly fair of him to arouse her like that and then leave her aching with frustration the way she was now. But she would not stoop to begging him to make love against his will.

"It has been a long day," she said in a brittle little voice. "Good night."

Before he could answer, she turned abruptly and entered her stateroom, leaving him standing in the corridor outside. The expression on his face was branded into her brain and brought a wave of anguish that blotted out Megan's righteous anger. Along with the apology and regret, she saw that same hint of shame she had detected during their heated exchange the night before when Case had told her he didn't have to trick women into his bed. Dear God, she didn't want him to feel *guilty* about not wanting to go to bed with her. She didn't want him to feel sorry for her. She just wanted him to *want* her the way he once had.

Sagging with her despondency, Megan discovered that she was suddenly tired right down to the marrow of her bones. But even as she undressed listlessly and got into bed, she suspected that sleep wouldn't come any time soon. There was too much to think about and try to understand. And there was also that vague physical ache low in her pelvis that she knew to be sexual frustration. With a brief flare of vengeance, she hoped Case was having trouble going to sleep, too. Then she relived the intense scene with him at the edge of the pier, felt again his passion with its edge of desperation, and knew without a doubt he *had* wanted her as much as she had wanted him. Why then had he pulled away, not just literally but mentally? Why hadn't he wanted to resume their lovemaking here on the yacht? Megan was unable to answer that question, but it plagued her for some time before she was finally able to sleep.

The next morning she was awakened by the sound of human voices and movements around the boat. She lay there several moments, telling herself she wasn't as tired as she felt. When she suddenly realized the boat was moving quite briskly through the water and not at anchor, it was the impetus she needed to get her out of bed. Today they were sailing to their next anchorage at Tobago Cays. She didn't want to lie down here in her stateroom and miss her first sail on a yacht.

Peering out a porthole, she saw a blue and golden world that beckoned her to come outside. Hastily she donned one of her new bikinis, a vibrant blue one that echoed the color of her eyes. Checking her appearance in the mirror on the door of her tiny bathroom, she was reassured that at age thirty-two after having borne two children, she still had a tiny waist, slim hips, and firm shapely thighs. Her high breasts curved temptingly out of the top of the skimpy bikini bra.

Wrinkling up her nose as she noted the ivory hue of her skin, Megan slipped on a long-sleeved blue-

and-white striped cover-up and got her sunglasses and the tube of cream advertised to block out all the harmful rays of the sun while promoting a golden-brown tan. Outside she issued a cheerful greeting to everyone in general and settled herself into a corner of the cockpit, making every effort just to stay out of the way.

Case was behind the wheel steering while Jacques and Alina took care of raising and trimming the sails. Megan couldn't keep back a gasp of fright as the boat tilted farther and farther over on its side, making it difficult for her even to stay seated on the high side, where she happened to be. She knew sailboats were supposed to heel, but the sensation was strange. Experiencing a motion vicariously on the screen and in photographs and actually *feeling* it were two different things. The brisk wind sent the boat surging through the waves at a speed she found somewhat dizzying.

Since nobody else appeared in the least concerned, Megan tried to suppress her uneasiness. Case had a broad grin on his face as he watched Jacques move about with loose-limbed ease up on the foredeck. Alina smiled as though everything were fine and went down inside the boat, saying something about *petit déjeuner,* which Megan knew was French for breakfast. Deciding that she would be more comfortable on the opposite side, she executed the move with a great deal of caution and then relaxed enough to take in her surroundings. Behind them was the rich verdure of St. Vincent and Young Island, no separation between them discernible at this distance and perspective. Up ahead the schooner cut through the blue waves, and one by one its sails fluttered aloft and filled with wind.

"Oh! Isn't it beautiful!" Megan exclaimed, enchanted with the grace and symmetry of the scene as the old-fashioned vessel sailed along, with the clear water like liquid crystal breaking at its bow.

Megan looked around at Case, eager for his agreement as a kind of proof that he was sharing her sense of wonder. He had stood up, turning the helm over to Jacques, who had returned to the cockpit to join them.

"Perfect," Case said in a satisfied voice, looking past Megan at the schooner with narrowed, assessing eyes. "The sun should be right in another half hour or so."

Megan had to clench her jaws closed to keep back a disgruntled retort. Was it really asking too much of Case for him to enjoy a wonderful moment with her and forget about work for only a brief spell? She thought not. With him it was just *work, work, work.*

"Are we close enough?" Jacques was asking.

"For the time being," Case replied. "Later I'll want to get closer and get some shots of Marcelle on deck."

While he and Jacques discussed the plans for the day's photographing, Megan smothered her irritation and watched Case out of the corner of her eye. He stood in the cockpit with one foot braced on the edge of her seat, his body swaying in tune with the boat's forward surges. In dark green shorts and a short-sleeved shirt unbuttoned down the front, his feet clad in leather moccasins, he looked rugged and masculine and thoroughly at ease. The brisk breeze ruffled his beard and blew tendrils of hair across his forehead. Taking note of the power suggested in his muscled thighs and his deep chest with its heavy covering of dark hair, Megan felt a sharp stir of sexual awareness and tilted her head back against the cabin top, glad of the protection of her oversized sunglasses. Last night's frustration had returned full force.

"Meg. You okay?"

Case's inquiry brought her eyes open and she saw that he was looking at her with a concerned frown. Evidently he had thought she might be seasick.

"I'm fine," she said brightly and turned to take the plate Alina was handing her from the open hatchway. On it was a generous slice of dark bread with butter melting on top and fresh pineapple cut into bite-sized pieces. The cup fitted into the plate was partially filled with steaming, fragrant coffee.

Much to her surprise Megan discovered she was hungry and able to eat every morsel of her breakfast in spite of the unfamiliar motion. Afterward when Alina smilingly refused an offer of help in cleaning up, Megan took off her cover-up in preparation for sunbathing. Aware of Case's close observation while she applied sunscreen cream to her bare white skin, she made quite a leisurely process of it, glancing up finally and letting her gaze intersect with his.

"Better take it easy," he advised. "You know how easily you burn."

His eyes said much more as they lingered on the

curves of her breasts exposed to view by the bikini top and then slid lower to the provocatively brief panties that hid precious little of the shapely feminine form he had caressed in the darkness of the pier the previous night.

"I do know," Megan replied in a deeply satisfied voice and stretched out like a cat, languid in the warm rays of the sun.

After that, he seemed to be totally unaware of her existence as he became engrossed in his work. Using various lenses and moving from one part of the boat to another, he took picture after picture of the schooner under sail, a task that was anything but easy under the circumstances. From time to time he would emit a curse when the boat would hit an unexpectedly large wave and threaten his balance or spoil the shot he was about to take.

Megan could feel his nerves winding tighter and tighter. Occasionally she would suggest he should take a break, but got no more than a frown or an abstracted glance for her trouble. After sunning on her back for a long while—she wasn't sure exactly how long since she wasn't wearing her wristwatch—she turned over on her stomach and dozed off, grumbling mentally that the day could have been perfect if only Case would relax and enjoy himself a little more. She didn't understand why he had to concentrate so single-mindedly on work. No wonder he didn't enjoy his travel assignments.

By noon Case finally decided he had taken enough shots of the schooner from a distance while it was under sail. He stepped down into the cockpit and sat down just as Alina was handing out a big wicker tray of sandwiches and chilled bottles of beer. Taking one of the sandwiches, he bit into it hungrily and took a deep swig of beer. He had taken off the shirt and already his shoulders, chest, and legs had begun to darken.

"We'd better turn on the engine and get closer now," he told Jacques, who got up at once and went down below.

Megan could hear the Frenchman as he radioed the schooner and talked in rapid French. Then the diesel engine rumbled into life, disrupting the quiet and causing the seat underneath Megan to vibrate. She couldn't contain her irritation any longer.

"I don't see what the big hurry is," she said peevishly. "Couldn't we just relax a few minutes and have a leisurely lunch instead of this mad rush?"

"The big hurry is that I have a job to do," Case snapped back at her. "That's the only reason I'm here—remember?" He glared at her irritably and then seemed suddenly to come aware that she still wore nothing but the scanty bikini.

"You'd better get some clothes on if you know what's good for you," he said brusquely. "I'd be willing to bet it's already too late."

Megan lifted her chin to an obstinate angle, but it wasn't long before she followed his advice. As soon as lunch was over she donned the long-sleeved cover-up and then went down to her stateroom for white cotton slacks and a big-brimmed hat. Her skin was uncomfortably hot underneath the clothing, giving her the awful intuition that Case was right. She might have overdone her first day in the open sunlight. It was bad enough to contemplate sunburn, but she would probably also have to put up with Case's "I told you so."

Chapter Six

*M*egan was right on one count and wrong on the other: She *was* sunburned but Case didn't say "I told you so," as he would have had a legitimate right to do. Instead he blamed himself for not having reminded her sooner to cover up.

By the time it became apparent to both of them that she was indeed burned from her exposure to the tropical sun, Megan's state of mind was such that she could have taken just about anything in stride. They had arrived in Tobago Cays that afternoon, the name designating four small islands. It was a beautiful unspoiled location with no human habitations in sight, just other yachts that had arrived before them. Jacques had explained on the way that the spot was renowned among divers and snorkelers the world over for its phenomenal Horse Shoe Reef.

"Guess I'll have to wait until tomorrow to take some underwater pictures," Case remarked philosophically.

"Yes, you will need more sunlight," Jacques agreed readily.

This exchange took place after the anchor had been set and the four of them were sitting in the cockpit, shaded by a large awning and sipping a delicious concoction of fresh fruit juices Alina had prepared. Megan kept to herself the disgruntled reflection that there seemed plenty enough sunlight for the other people in the anchorage to enjoy themselves, those fortunate individuals who didn't have to think of work every second. She watched wistfully as dinghies plied back and forth between the yachts swinging at anchor and the various beaches on the cluster of small islands. Two wind-surfers with sails as brilliant as the primary colors on an artist's palette skimmed along out some distance from the anchored yachts. Now and again they would topple over and then right themselves again.

Expelling her breath noiselessly in a little sigh, Megan administered a scolding to her errant inner self. She was guilty of wanting too much, the opportunity to meet the challenge of this job and establish herself professionally *and* all the carefree fun of vacationing in the beautiful Caribbean. Case had tried to impress upon her from the outset that this trip was all work, and heaven knows, so far he had been every inch the working professional, even today when taking photographs aboard a moving boat had taxed his physical and mental endurance to the limit. In his place she would probably be tired, too, and willing to lounge comfortably and not itch to explore those green and white shorelines of the little islands, as she longed to do.

"How about it, Meg?" his voice broke into her reflections. "Want to give snorkeling a try this afternoon?"

Megan started, not believing her ears. She had tuned out the conversation in a spirit of resignation.

"I'd love to!" she exclaimed excitedly, sitting bolt upright.

"I would suggest you wear a shirt over your swimming suit and canvas shoes to protect your feet," Jacques advised, turning on Megan an indulgent smile. He went on to explain that since they would be snorkeling just offshore in the place he would take them, the water was quite shallow and the coral formations sometimes hazardously close to the surface. There was a danger of grazing the skin, but with shoes on, one could stand up if one wished or push off into deeper spots.

Megan immediately went below to her stateroom. When she had shed her long-sleeved cover-up and slacks, she caught sight of herself in the mirror on the bathroom door and grimaced at the rosy hue of her skin. She *had* gotten a little too much sun, but she didn't have time to waste on regrets for her folly.

Jacques and Alina took them in the dinghy to a sandy beach with dense growth of broad-leaved sea grapes.

"It is good here and the current is not dangerous,"

Jacques assured them and then left, promising to return in an hour and a half.

Megan had some difficulty at first learning to breathe through the snorkel, but once she mastered the technique, she quickly became enthralled with the underwater world she was able to see beneath her as she glided over the top of the water. It was such a quiet, mysterious world, inhabited by fish of breathtakingly beautiful colors and exotic shapes as well as other sea creatures. The sea urchins at first seemed especially sinister, ebony balls of sharp spikes nestled on the ocean floor among the coral formations, but they never seemed to move and the fish apparently took little notice of them. Nor of her, for that matter.

At first, Megan would find a solid footing every few minutes and stand up to look around and locate Case, since it would be possible to lose one's bearings and float off out of sight. But each time she would find him only a few yards away, so she stopped worrying about getting lost, confident that Case was somehow keeping an eye on her.

Her favorite fish were broad and flat with transparent frilly fins along their back, the color a gorgeous, soul-satisfying gentian blue with darker purple spots that seemed to glow with phosphorescent light. They hovered here and there, letting her come close before they would dart away. And then she floated over a whole school of them and gazed down in awe at the inexpressible beauty of the combination of grace, symmetry, and color. She found herself wishing that Case could see this, too, since words would never describe it adequately. Almost as soon as the wish was formed, she turned her head slightly sideways and saw that he was close beside her, his arm extended downward, the hand pointing in a kind of silent communication.

Megan was like a child greedy for more and more pleasure, never wanting the wonderful fun to end, but even as she grew increasingly adept in moving about over the water, learning how to use her hands and legs to make herself stop and hover over one spot or put on a burst of speed to follow a quarry, she was aware the whole time that the sun was going farther down. The fascinating underwater world grew more and more shadowy. When she felt as well as heard the buzz of an outboard coming closer, she knew Jacques had come back for them and turned reluctantly back toward the beach, bubbling over with her enthusiasm when she surfaced and walked over to the two men, who were waiting for her.

"It was so *wonderful!*" she told Jacques and then turned eagerly to Case. "Did you see the striped ones?" she demanded. "Some of them were half electric blue and half shimmering gold. Some others were part red and part gold—"

He grinned and nodded that he had seen them.

"How about that long, skinny shy fellow who was so obviously hiding—did you see him?" Case wanted to know.

Megan said that she had and suggested almost sympathetically that maybe he was embarrassed that he was so brown and plain among the more flamboyant varieties of fish life.

"And the *coral!*" she went on wonderingly. "It's

so *weird* and fascinating. All the different varieties and shapes and formations. That brain coral *does* look like a human brain, doesn't it? Oh, I just can't wait to come back tomorrow!"

She knew she was prattling on like a child during the ride in the dinghy back to the yacht, but Jacques seemed pleased with her enthusiasm, as though she were complimenting some personal possession of his. And Case agreed with her in spirit even though the masculine personality wouldn't permit such effusive expression. He commented regretfully that he wished he had been able to take pictures.

Megan didn't take offense, because she thought he was speaking with the inbred photographer's urge to capture his most noteworthy experiences on film, not from any feeling of guilt or regret that he hadn't gotten good pictures for the magazine feature that afternoon.

Noticing her withered and wrinkled hand, she held it up for general inspection.

"Look at this! I've been in the water so long I look like an old woman!"

The innocent remark brought the close scrutiny of both men, not just to her hand but to her face and her exposed arms and legs. Megan followed their gaze and noticed for the first time the changed color of her thighs, an angry red like a fresh welt. She knew immediately that the sensitive flesh underneath her knit pullover would be the same color if not darker.

"I should have listened to you, Case," she said quickly before he had a chance to speak. "Looks like I got a humdinger of a sunburn."

Case frowned, looking worried and vaguely angry.

"I was so damned busy today trying to get a decent shot when nothing would stay still for more than half a second, I just forgot about you sitting there in the sun," he apologized gravely, as though the whole thing were his fault rather than hers. "Jacques, do we have something good for sunburn on the boat?"

Jacques assured him that they did.

As soon as they had arrived at the anchored yacht and climbed aboard, Case peeled off his wet T-shirt and hung it over a lifeline to dry. Megan hesitated, wishing she could keep hers on, but it was sopping wet. Before she even pulled it clear of her head, she heard Case's muttered curse and knew he was looking at her sun-reddened skin. Glancing down at the beet-red hue of her chest and stomach, she tried to make a joke of it.

"No wonder the fish weren't scared of me," she wisecracked with forced humor. "They thought I was some new colorful species."

"Take a cool shower and I'll put something on it," Case ordered sternly, not amused. Megan didn't argue, thinking to herself as she went below to her stateroom that he looked like a disapproving parent too concerned about an injury to scold the errant child.

Carefully removing the sodden bikini, Megan winced as she saw the vivid contrast between white and red skin. But touching herself, she found her skin wasn't painfully sore and took some consolation in that fact. If Jacques had a really good ointment aboard as he had indicated he did, maybe she would heal quickly and not peel.

Megan had showered as instructed and was patting herself dry with a towel when Case tapped twice on the door of her stateroom and walked in without waiting for a summons. He took a long appraising look at her naked body and shook his head soberly before tossing the tube he held onto her bunk and coming over to take the towel away from her.

"Turn around," he ordered.

Megan obeyed meekly, feeling even more strongly than before like an erring child before the figure of authority. This wasn't quite the situation she would have liked when Case was seeing her naked for the first time in two years. She was anything but sexy. If he hadn't wanted to make love to her last night, there wasn't a chance he would want to now.

"Okay," he said in a gentler tone when he had patted her dry with such care she hadn't felt a twinge of discomfort. He tossed the towel into the compact bathroom. "Now lie down and I'll put some of this cream on you."

Megan lay first on her stomach so that he could attend to her back. The ointment felt ice cold, causing her to gasp aloud with the first shock of it on her fevered flesh. But then it felt wonderful. She sighed, relaxing totally under the tender, unhurried application. Even as she reminded herself there was nothing faintly sexual in what he was doing, she felt a telltale vague ache in her lower pelvis.

"Now. Turn over," he instructed when he had

spread the marvelous cooling ointment all over her shoulders and back and the entire length of the backs of her legs.

Megan rolled over, her breathing shallow and fast for no good reason and her nipples hardening underneath his close gaze. *Don't be silly,* she chided herself weakly. *He's only being kind. He won't find you in the least sexy looking like this.* But as his dark gaze collided with hers a long moment, Megan wasn't so sure she was telling herself the truth, and that tinge of uncertainty made it impossible for her to control her reflexive responses to the touch of his hands.

Her breasts and her thighs and her stomach simply could not believe there was no sexual promise in the rhythmic stroke of his fingers against her flesh. The excited nerves just below the surface of her soothed skin radioed messages that caused her heart to beat faster and send the blood pulsing through her veins. She was almost sure he must be able to feel the pulsation under his fingertips and know her high level of stimulation.

"There. Feel any better?"

Case found the cap and put it back on the tube.

"Much better." Megan was sensitive to the husky seduction in her voice. It heightened her arousal and increased the suspense of the moment as she waited for him to look at her and show her what he was feeling by the expression in his eyes. "Thank you," she added when it seemed to be taking forever for him to screw on the cap.

Case glanced quickly toward her face, his eyes

searching hers. When he stood up abruptly, Megan had to bite back her protest. How could he leave her like this? But then she realized he wasn't leaving the stateroom. He was washing his hands in the little basin in the bathroom, drying them on the towel he'd thrown on the floor, coming back and sitting on the side of the bunk.

"You're sure it feels better? You're not just saying that?" he asked hesitantly, his eyes on his fingers as they touched the ruddy tops of her breasts, sliding along the full curves with such tantalizing gentleness that her nipples contracted into hard aching knots. Megan arched her back instinctively as though to thrust them up to him.

"I really mean it," she managed to murmur as he bent over slowly and kissed first one hard tip of a breast and then the other. She drew in her breath sharply as he worried one nipple very tenderly with his tongue. "I don't feel . . . any pain . . . at all . . ." The disclaimer ended in a moan. His hands were cupping her breasts tenderly, holding the sensitive weight while he sucked gently and traced warm, wet circles with his tongue. Megan brought her hands up to his head and eased her fingers into the thickness of his hair as though compelled to touch him but not wanting to do anything sudden that would distract him from his preoccupation or make him stop.

When he transferred his attention to the other breast and flicked the tip of his tongue back and forth across the rocklike nipple, white-hot sensations shot through her, and Megan groaned his name aloud, writhing her buttocks against the coolness of the sheet under her. One of his hands seemed to receive the desperation of the message her lower torso was sending and reluctantly left the breast it held, first tracing the rich undercurve before slipping down along the shape of her waist and hip and outer thigh. As though giving fair warning of his presence at the door of her woman's citadel, Case caressed first one soft inner thigh and then the other until Megan thought she would die with the waiting. When she couldn't withstand another second of delay, his palm settled on the furry, aching mound between her legs. She moaned and closed her thighs to crush the hand closer.

"Case, I'll just die if you don't make love to me," she whispered, running her hands urgently across the breadth of his shoulders.

At her words he went still for a moment, his mouth warm upon her breast. Megan wondered if she might have imagined the hesitation when he resumed kissing and teasing the breast and the hand between her legs pressed and kneaded while one finger plunged boldly into her velvet wetness, making her forget everything but her throbbing need. It had been so long since she had given in to her passion there was no room for the rational, no time to halt him and say, "No, not this way."

Case knew her body too well, and with the skillful, knowledgeable invasion of his hand, he brought her to climax, one shuddering paroxysm following another until she lay quiescent, his face burrowed between her breasts.

"I can always satisfy you, Meg . . . somehow," he murmured against her, talking to himself more than to her, it seemed.

The words raised an alarm inside Megan she didn't understand. Grasping his head between her two hands, she raised it and forced his eyes to come level with hers.

"What do you mean by that, Case? Just now, why *didn't* you—I mean, don't you *want* to . . ." She found it impossible to continue what had been an incoherent effort to voice her question. The expression on his face deepened her sense of something being terribly wrong, something he was ashamed to tell her. "Case, you've got to tell me," she pleaded in a scared little voice. "Whatever it is, I've got to know." Even if hearing the truth meant learning that he simply could not bear making love to her anymore, she had to know where she stood with him.

Case reached up and took her hands away from his head. Moving with the stiff deliberation of someone much older than his thirty-eight years, he straightened and sat on the side of the bunk, not looking at her.

"You can't expect a man just to jump—" he began tersely and then broke off. "Two years is a long time," he began again in a different voice but one equally as evasive, the note of apology and pleading just as bewildering to Megan as his initial belligerence. "Can't you just give me a little *time*, Meg?"

Megan felt a chill of fear drifting over her skin and shivered as she drew her knees up close to her chest, curling her body in upon itself for protection from the unnamed threat of whatever was wrong.

"Time for what, Case?" she asked fearfully. "It's been two years for me, too, and I want you physically now as much as I ever did—" She broke off, recoiling as Case's head snapped around and he glared at her angrily.

"So you still want me *physically*," he bit out savagely. "Well, you might just be out of luck."

Megan stared back at him, her confused mind grappling to deal with his words and the fury in his tone. He sounded as though he *hated* her.

"Is this some kind of punishment, Case?" she asked uncertainly, not wanting to provoke him further. "Are you so angry at me because I wouldn't give up my job . . ." Megan had never felt stranger or more unable to read the situation in which she found herself. She watched with growing puzzlement and suspense as Case underwent another marked change. For a moment she thought he was going to admit she was right in her attempt to explain his reaction, but then he shook his head violently as though to clear it and turned away from her, bending over and resting his elbows on his knees, fatigue and discouragement in the slope of his wide shoulders, the droop of his head. His gaze was fixed on the floor as he spoke.

"What the hell's the use of lying. I might as well tell you the truth and get it all out in the open. After all, it's not the kind of thing a man can hide for long." He stopped, aware that Megan had stiffened behind him.

"Case! You're not saying—" She bit off the horrified denial and waited for him to make assurances that didn't come. "I mean, we *always*—that is, there was never *anything* wrong—" Finding the going more awkward that she could ever have imagined, Megan swallowed and gathered her courage. "Case, are you telling me you think you might be impotent?"

He nodded.

Megan stared at the back of his head, her breast flooded by an amalgam of powerful emotions that struck her mute and passive until she could deal with them. A fierce love and understanding sympathy made her want to take him in her arms and tell him unequivocally there was nothing wrong with him. She wouldn't *allow* him to have anything wrong with him that could render him so miserable. And yet, he was admitting he had at least *tried* to make love to other women. He had been unfaithful to her! That inescapable fact called up a sense of bitterness and betrayal. Megan was so torn she didn't know what to say to him, what to *do* . . .

"I wanted you so much last night," Case was saying in a bleak, resigned voice. "But I was afraid the same thing might happen with *you*—" He stopped at the sound of her sharply indrawn breath, well aware that he was hanging himself in more ways than one with this confession. Steeling his courage, he continued.

"I didn't want to take the chance of disappointing you, of spoiling the chance, however slim, that you might be thinking of coming back to me."

Megan got up, slipped on a nylon peignoir that felt cool against her skin, and sat next to Case on the edge of the bunk.

"I'm trying to think about this from your point of view, Case," she said with forced calm. "I'm trying like *hell* not to be jealous, but it's hard. Terribly hard. I guess I knew that in two years' time you were bound to go to bed with other women, but—Oh, Case, I wish I didn't know for *sure!*" she cried out unhappily.

Case raised his head and looked into her face, his face ravaged with his own emotion but his gaze unwaveringly honest.

"I was so angry at you, Meg," he said soberly. "I think I had some notion I was getting back at you for not wanting me as much as you wanted that damned job." He laughed grimly. "The joke was really on me, though, as things turned out. Then I started wondering what my problem was, whether I just didn't want to make love to any other woman besides you or whether I had something physical wrong with me. Before long, I wasn't even certain you *had* been satisfied all along. After all, a woman can pretend."

"*No,* Case, I *never* pretended—I never *had* to!" Megan assured him earnestly. "Sex had nothing to do with the reason I wouldn't give up my job the way you insisted. I just wanted to *do* something completely on my own, *be* somebody in my own right. If only you could understand that."

The familiar stubborn expression settled over Case's features.

"You *were* somebody, as far as I was concerned.

You were my wife. You were the mother of our children. But that wasn't enough, was it? It's not enough now."

He didn't really have to wait for an answer. He already knew it. Case felt himself sinking deeper into the despair that at times was almost more than he could bear. If he had failed to give her everything she wanted before, when he had been confident of his sexual prowess, what chance did he have now?

"Case, you just *won't* try to understand, will you?"

Megan's voice shook slightly with the sadness and the frustration inside her. It seemed there was just no hope she and Case would get back together and solve all the problems between them. He wouldn't listen to her. Right this moment she was sure there was nothing physical wrong with him, but what was the use in trying to convince him? His face and his whole bearing were closed against her.

"I think I'll snatch a little rest before time for supper," Case announced stiffly, getting up without looking at her.

Megan sighed, her shoulders sagging with discouragement. "Maybe I will, too," she said tiredly. "Thanks again for tending to my sunburn." The tinge of irony in her voice reminded both of them that he had tended to more than sunburn.

After he had left, she lay down on her bunk, pondering what had happened between them and what had been said, a deep feeling of guilt growing inside her as she gave the only possible explanation to what Case had just so shamefully revealed to her. Obviously his sense of rejection, growing out of their separation, was so severe he had come to doubt his manhood, as incredible as that notion was to Megan, as incredible as it would undoubtedly be to any woman who came in contact with him. He was virile and masculine as only a strong, decisive man can be. Yet, unseen to the feminine eye, his libido had suffered serious wounds.

Weighed down with a sense of hopelessness over this latest complication in the tangled web of the relationship between herself and Case, Megan drifted into a groggy sleep, her mind full of seemingly unanswerable questions. How could she ever undo the damage she had unknowingly done to him? How could they ever get back together and be happy?

Some time later she awoke to the sound of Case's laughter coming from outside in the cockpit. It brought a resurgence of optimism to her breast as she got up and dressed. As long as there was laughter, there was a chance of healing wounds, whether they be physical or psychic.

"I see you started the cocktail hour without me!" she accused gaily as she stepped out into the capacious cockpit where Case was sitting with Jacques and Alina.

"We were thinking perhaps you would not ever join us," Jacques teased in his musical accent, standing immediately and then going down inside the boat to make her a drink.

Megan settled herself comfortably at the opposite end of the long seat on which Case lounged, a tall glass in his hand. She was aware that each of them was eyeing the other as surreptitiously as possible, the earlier scene hanging between them and creating a wall of awkwardness. Megan thought to herself that no one looking at him now would give any credence to his fears about his virility. He sat sprawled back with one bare foot resting on the edge of the seat, the light fabric of his slacks pulled tight across the masculine bulge of his crotch and the powerful muscles of his thighs. The loose chambray shirt failed to hide the breadth of his shoulders or the depth of his chest. The hands cradling his glass, brown from the sun now, were both strong and sensitive. Balled into a fist, they could easily knock a man down, and yet the fingers were adept at making the fine adjustments on a complicated camera, adept also at touching a woman's body . . .

"My sunburn is better," Megan blurted self-consciously, stirred by her own thoughts and aware of his oblique gaze on her arms and legs, covered by cool cotton slacks and a long-sleeved blouse.

"Good. I'm glad." He sounded as if he meant his words, but at the same time his voice firmly refused to admit he was thinking about anything else but her sunburn.

Jacques stepped back into the cockpit, holding out a tinkling glass of rum punch for Megan.

"Has Case told you of our plans for this evening?" he asked, and reading the answer in her face, denial and immediate curiosity, continued. "We thought we would have a—what do you Americans call it?—a 'cookout' on the beach."

An excited grin broke out over Megan's face.

"What fun!" she exclaimed. Then as a thought

occurred to her she glanced over inquiringly at Case and then out at the anchored schooner. Were the other members of the magazine crew included?

Case shook his head.

"Jacques and Alina are inviting the two of us to have dinner with them on the beach rather than with the others on the schooner," he explained carefully, as though simply giving information. "They scouted out a place this afternoon while you and I were snorkeling." He hesitated. "It's up to you. I told Jacques you might not be up to roughing it."

Reading between the lines, Megan knew he was telling her he hadn't been sure she would want to be paired with him in a cozy foursome, not after what he had told her that afternoon.

"Sure I'm up to it," she insisted enthusiastically, pulling her legs up under her and sitting crosslegged on the seat. "It sounds like great fun!"

Anticipation put a sparkle in her blue eyes and curved her lips in a pert smile as she took a sweeping view around her and saw nothing to threaten her wonderful mood. In the mellow light of late afternoon the sea was a deep sapphire blue. The shorelines of the two islands she could see from where she sat were a lush, velvety green rimmed with purest white. The breeze ruffled her hair and cooled her warm skin, bringing with it faint laughter and the muted ring of happy voices from the other anchored yachts. All this and the company of the man she loved on what promised to be yet another Caribbean adventure: a cookout on the beach!

"It sounds like great fun," she said again, smiling

happily at Case, wanting to share with him the feeling that her heart was brimming full of warm emotions, primary among them optimism for the future. There was nothing sexually wrong with him. She was sure of it. If he would only give her a chance to prove it, she would . . . that very night.

Chapter Seven

Jacques took Megan and Case to the beach first, instructing them to find large pieces of driftwood to sit on while he went back to the yacht for Alina and the rest of the food. Upon his return he dug a small pit in the sand and started a charcoal fire to grill the fish, bought from native fishermen that very afternoon and wrapped in heavy foil. There would also be small whole potatoes, roasted on the coals, and salad that Alina had made up ahead of time, a mixture of crisp lettuce and avocado and giant capers. She would pour the dressing over it at the last minute.

While the fish and potatoes cooked, the tantalizing odors heightening their appetites, they sat on the pieces of driftwood, sipping chilled white wine from plastic glasses and carrying on an impromptu lesson in French and English.

"Sand," Megan would pronounce carefully, picking up a silken handful near her bare feet and letting it sift through her fingers.

"Sand," Alina would repeat laughingly and then give the translation in her language. Megan would practice the French word until her pronunciation satisfied Alina, and then it was Alina's turn to pick a word.

The mood was one of total relaxation and hilarity. By the time they were ready to eat, Megan reflected to herself that she couldn't have felt more at ease with another couple, even if she had known them for years. And never before in her life had she tasted more delicious food.

The four individual fish were cooked whole with the heads on and flavored with some subtle blend of herbs and fresh lemon slices. The salad dressing was tangy with garlic and vinegar and red wine, a perfect complement to the crisp salad. The potatoes were cooked perfectly, flaky and tender with crisp outer skins. For a while, everyone was too devoted to eating to allow time for conversation except for fervent compliments and wholehearted agreement.

Afterward, when they had cleaned up, covering the burned-out coals with sand and putting all the debris in a plastic garbage bag they had brought along for the purpose, Jacques persuaded Alina to sing for them. It turned out she had a lovely, husky voice that made shivers run over Megan's skin. Most of the songs seemed to be sad ones, the liquid strangeness of the lyrics making them even more poignant.

"That was beautiful," Megan murmured after Alina had stopped singing and the four of them sat encased in a hushed silence.

The peaceful spell held them in its grip as they loaded up the dinghy and returned to the yacht, Megan and Alina climbing aboard on the first trip while Jacques and Case went back to get what they hadn't been able to fit into the small boat. Alina set about at once making a pot of coffee, and then she and Megan together washed and dried and put away the dirty dishes. By the time the two men returned, Alina had gotten out cups and brandy snifters and a bottle of French cognac.

"*Cafe?*" she offered to everyone in general.

"Not for me," Case refused, but he did accept a snifter of cognac.

Megan didn't really want either coffee or cognac, but she asked for half a cup of the strong, black coffee and sipped it slowly, feeling the nervousness build up inside her with each swallow. Before long they all would be going to bed and she would be faced with enacting the plan she'd been building in her mind all evening. Now that the time for carrying it out was near, she was suffering all kinds of qualms that threatened to erode her nerve. What if the whole thing backfired on her?

The conversation was desultory and soon punctuated by audible yawns. Looking around the anchorage, Megan saw that most of the other boats were dark now except for the wink of anchor lights. It was a scene to lull one to sleep if one weren't coiled tight with conflicting determination and apprehension. Unable to sit there in the cockpit and wait until someone else broke up the gathering, she stretched and faked a yawn.

"If this is a contest on who can hold out the longest, then I lose," she announced cheerfully. "The whole evening was wonderful, but I'm falling asleep sitting here."

To her relief, her words seemed to be the signal the others were waiting for. Minutes later in her stateroom, Megan lay in her bunk and listened as the quiet sounds of movement died away and silence settled over the yacht until the ripple of water against the hull and the breeze gusting through the rigging gradually seemed to become louder. Megan could feel the pulsebeat in her body as her nervousness reached an uncomfortable level and she waged war with herself.

Why don't you wait until another night? the coward in her advised.

Another night won't be any better than this one, answered the voice of her resolution.

But he's probably already asleep. Sex is the last thing on his mind right now.

I can wake him. I can put sex on his mind.

What if he doesn't want you?

He does want me—I know he does.

Megan got up quickly from the bunk, afraid to stay there longer and listen to the inner debate. Quietly she grasped the handle on her stateroom door and turned it slowly, taking care to make no noise and then easing the door open and closing it behind her with the same deliberate caution. Her heart was pounding in her breast as she crossed the narrow passageway to the door of Case's stateroom and hesitated there a long moment, breathing deeply and summoning her courage. When she had slipped inside and closed the door noiselessly behind her, the charged silence in the darkness told her he was awake and startled at her entry.

"Case?" she whispered, the sound a mere wisp as it squeezed past her tight throat.

"What the hell do you think you're doing?" he growled back in a savage undertone.

Megan almost gave in to her cowardly impulses without any further struggle, and she probably would have if her intentions had been solely to administer sexual therapy. But she realized suddenly that she wasn't there in his stateroom just to ease an unwarranted fear from his mind, although she did hope to accomplish that end. She was also there because she ached to have him make love to her. It was as though she had been gradually starving for his lovemaking and affection over a two-year period of time until suddenly her hunger had reached desperate proportions. This sudden clarity of mind concerning her motivations erased all her doubts and let her concentrate her full powers of persuasion upon the man lying there in tense silence in the darkness.

"Since you won't come to my stateroom, I decided I would come to yours," she whispered, moving over to his bunk and sitting on the edge. Her hands were so eager to reach for him and touch him, she had to discipline them sternly and bid them wait for the right time.

"Case, if you've been trying to drive me crazy

these past few days, you've done a good job of it," she continued in the same husky, seductive tone. "Every time I look at you, I remember what it was like with us when we made love. I think about the way your body looked . . . *naked* . . ." Megan kept the word on her tongue, tasting and savoring it. She felt a tremor over the surface of her bare skin and shivered with her own arousal as she reached out slowly and touched him, her hand encountering his bare chest and feeling him tense and resistant. She was doing a fantastic job of turning herself on so far, but not him, it seemed.

Slowly she brought the other hand to his chest, too, and slid her palms across the hair-roughened contours, creating a friction of heat that burned her skin. Her confidence soared when one hand paused over his heart and felt the erratic drumbeat. At least he wasn't calm. Deliberately she slid lower, finding the sheet around his waist and stroking her fingertips just underneath it as though it would take her a thousand years to work her way to her obvious destination.

"Meg—"

He groaned her name out in a kind of mixed plea and protest at the same time that he reached for her, his hands closing hard around her shoulders and pulling her down to him. Megan went willingly, fitting her body pliantly on top of his and settling her hips languidly over the jutting evidence that he was as aroused already as she was. Her passion rose swiftly as Case took the back of her head in one large hand and pressed her head down to him, his mouth taking hers hungrily, his lips meshing hard with hers, his tongue thrusting into the hot sweetness of her mouth and finding her tongue arched and ready to couple with his. In further devastation of her senses, Case used his free hand to explore her naked length stretched on top of him.

No longer a conscious seductress but just a woman inflamed by her need, Megan couldn't remain still a second. When Case stroked her buttocks and the backs of her thighs, she writhed her upper torso from side to side across his chest, rubbing her hard nipples against the hairy roughness, and writhed her pelvis against his, as though trying to accommodate the thrusting maleness through the barrier of the sheet. Against his lips she murmured his name in an expression of the urgency of her need.

Then abruptly Case was rolling her over on her back and tearing aside the offending sheet, his body shaking with the frenzy of his great passion and his breath coming in labored gusts as he positioned himself on top of her and without any apology for the suddenness, thrust deep inside her as though his very life depended upon immediate consummation. Megan gave a little strangled cry that mixed with the deep groan torn out of the very core of his being. Case held his breath and lay dead still a long moment, managing to keep at bay the paroxysm that threatened far too soon.

Megan wrapped her arms and her legs around him, drawing him closer, keeping him deep inside her, wishing irrationally they could stay this close forever. But then that thought was disrupted and gone when Case pulled a little out of her and drove deep again, his body wracked with tremors at the enormity of his effort to prolong the intensity of his passion. Again and again he thrust hard and deep, lifting her to higher and higher levels of sensation and thrilling her heart with the husky litany he murmured, telling her as he always had when they made love that she was his love, his life, his world.

Then suddenly the control was gone. They were left completely at the mercy of the storm of passion they had created together, crashing into wave after violent wave and cresting each one in utter breathlessness, being borne higher and higher from one level of exquisite torture to another even more unbearable until they plunged over the edge of the universe into oblivion.

Recovery was slow. At first they lay exactly as they were, as though it were enough for the moment to have landed at all without checking to see the damage. Finally, Case stirred, making Megan aware that she bore his heavy weight. As he rolled over she turned with him so that they lay still together on their sides. With his arms around her, cradling her close, she was flooded with an overwhelming contentment that was enough in itself for the moment without any intrusion of thought or any other emotion. Later they could talk, she just barely managed to tell herself before she drifted off to sleep.

Case held her, listening to her soft breathing and trying without success to keep himself immersed in the warm aftermath of passion where there was no thought, just total satiation. Why had Megan come in here tonight and seduced him into making love to her? That's precisely what she had done. If her motive had been to dispel his fear of impotency, she certainly had succeeded. Case had never been more aroused in his life, had never gone any higher, had never felt quite the same surging power of his male sexuality after a long period of abstinence imposed by his own self-doubt.

Or was this sudden overture after two years a power play staged in bed? Did Megan hope to establish that Case could be a man only with her and thus bring him back to her under her own terms?

Disquieted as he was by these suspicions, Case only hugged her a little closer to him, loving the feel of her in his arms, warm and soft and vulnerable in her sleep. With a sigh, he burrowed his face in her silky, fragrant hair and resolutely clicked his brain to "off" the way he would one of his cameras. Tonight he would hold her. Tomorrow he would try to sort out her motives.

Megan awoke some time later, disoriented at first but coming completely awake as she realized where she was and remembered what had happened with her and Case. The sound of his slow, regular breathing assured her he was asleep. Megan eased herself over on her back and tried to flex cramped muscles without disturbing him. As memory of his impassioned lovemaking flooded back she was stirred by deep tenderness and love and satisfaction for what had been clearly proved: There was nothing wrong with Case sexually. She had been so sure there wouldn't be.

Whatever problems he had experienced with other women must have had an emotional basis. How could Megan be other than glad that she might be the only woman who could make him happy? But if that were true, it only intensified the pressure upon her to work out matters between Case and herself. And yet how could she when he seemed so closed to reason?

With her mind working clearly, Megan felt her spirits drop as she faced the truth that tonight's lovemaking had changed nothing between herself and Case. There had never been any cause for dissatisfaction with the physical part of their marriage, but sex obviously wasn't everything. Tomorrow when he awoke, would Case still demand total capitulation from her? If so, she would be faced with the same difficult decision of whether she should try to be what he wanted: a contented housewife and devoted mother with no high-priority outside interests or career.

Shifting restlessly, Megan knew she was far from being able to go back to sleep, and there was little room in the bunk for tossing and turning without disturbing Case. Maybe it would be better for her to go back to her own stateroom where she could turn on a light and try to lull her mind with reading. Being careful not to wake Case, she climbed over him and eased silently out of his stateroom.

The muted click of the latch caused Case to start and then come partially awake. When he reached out and searched for Megan, he found nothing but a void next to him, the sheet still warm from her body. He realized then that he had been awakened by the stealthy sounds of her departure, which in his groggy state seemed just another manifestation of her basic rejection of him as her husband. She had brought her warmth in here briefly and then taken it away again, leaving him alone. As he turned over on his stomach, covering the spot where she had been, Case expelled a deep breath and sank back into the blackness of sleep, filled with a bleak sense of confronting odds he would never be able to overcome.

It was almost daylight when Megan finally went back to sleep. She had tried unsuccessfully to read and then had sat propped up in her bunk for hours, pad on her knees and pencil in hand, trying to make some headway in getting ideas on paper for the feature she had to write. So far she hadn't had a glimmer of inspiration, and going over the notes she had been taking didn't produce a single idea. But at least she got her mind off her marital dilemma and finally fell into a tired sleep.

When she awoke, it was to discover that half the day was nearly gone and she was alone on the yacht with Alina. Jacques and Case were gone with the dinghy, Case having left her to sleep while he went off to take underwater pictures of the reef. Megan had to suppress a crushing disappointment, even while her common sense told her it was all for the best. Her skin was still tender from yesterday's overexposure to the sun, and she would do well to protect it today and stay out of the direct rays.

After the previous evening there was no awkwardness between herself and Alina despite the language barrier. When the younger woman set about preparing lunch, Megan pitched in and helped, the two of them working companionably in the galley making a mouthwatering curried chicken salad and deviled eggs. They had the food cooling in the refrigerator, the galley spotlessly clean, when the two men returned.

"I could have cried when I woke up and found you'd gone without me this morning," Megan told Case ruefully. "I guess you knew it would be too big a temptation to snorkel again when I needed to stay out of the sun."

"I knocked on your stateroom door," Case replied so politely Megan's eyes widened in disbelief. "When you didn't answer, I took it to mean you preferred to sleep in."

Megan mulled over his cool tone and distant manner while he went down to his stateroom to change clothes. Why was he acting this way? No one overhearing the exchange between them just now would believe the two of them had made passionate love last night. In the light of day, did Case resent her for having crashed his defenses?

When he largely ignored her through lunch and maintained a careful distance throughout the remainder of the day, her mystification grew along with her exasperation. She made up her mind she would get to the bottom of the matter at the earliest opportunity, but it seemed that he deliberately avoided being alone with her.

After lunch Jacques pulled up anchor, as did the captain of the *Marie Antoinette,* and the two vessels sailed to the island of Union in order to clear customs and get permission to visit the lower Grenadines, which are owned and governed by Grenada rather than St. Vincent. During the sail Case sprawled comfortably in the cockpit, talking to Jacques the whole time while Megan stayed below out of the sun.

At Union everyone went ashore to a small open-air bar while the two captains went together to cope with the customs officials. It seemed to a rather disgruntled Megan that the three Frenchwomen closed in around Case like bees to a honey pot. The rapid flow of French words and phrases might elude her as far as their literal translation was concerned, but female flattery was recognizable in any language. Megan had to struggle to suppress her jealousy, even while her common sense told her Case was the only virile, attractive man present and the three Frenchwomen looked restless and bored.

Megan wandered away from the others to a large L-shaped concrete pool between the bar and the edge of the water. She watched several huge sea turtles and sharks move about in their limited space before deciding that she was acting childish, remaining aloof from the others just because Case was ignoring her. Still, it was such an effort to appear relaxed and sociable under the circumstances that she was immensely relieved when the two captains appeared, and it was time for the passengers to return to their respective vessels and get under sail immediately for the next anchorage at Petit St. Vincent, like Young Island an island owned by a luxury hotel.

"This looks like a popular place to anchor," Megan observed, coming up into the cockpit after they had reached their destination, the anchor had been set, and the awning put up. She looked around at the large number of yachts, some of them rivaling the *Marie Antoinette* in length and historical interest.

"It *is* very popular," Jacques affirmed. "The owners of the hotel are very friendly to cruising yachtsmen. Tonight you will hear many languages at the Jump-Up and see many different kinds of people."

"A *Jump-Up*," Megan repeated, thinking again that it was a strange name for the islands' version of disco she had heard so much about. Tonight the whole magazine crew would go ashore and attend a Jump-Up, but as was usually the case on this trip, their presence would be for the purpose of business as well as pleasure. It had been arranged with the management of the hotel for Case to take pictures, and Marcelle would be photographed in another of the designer ensembles.

Gazing ashore at the curving white line of sandy beach and the several little buildings with weathered sides and thatched roofs, Megan felt the inner thrill of anticipation returning. Looking further up into the green hills, she could glimpse here and there a cottage. Tonight would be another Caribbean adventure, a new kind of experience. She couldn't wait! And before it was over, she would find an opportunity to talk to Case and find out what was causing him to be so cold toward her.

As it turned out, the Jump-Up proved to be such fun that Megan didn't even have time to fret about not being able to get Case alone. First, there was the delightful novelty of the special currency one needed in order to purchase drinks at the bar, which was nothing more than a rude, two-sided shelter with a thatched roof, one of the buildings Megan had viewed from the yacht earlier that afternoon. Across from the bar was the "bank," a small wooden building with a porch across the front. There one exchanged East Caribbean money for "clams," bright yellow in color and reminding Megan of Monopoly money. Right in the middle of each bill was a cartoon depiction of a clam with "Our Leader" written underneath.

Then there was the captivating atmosphere of the gathering, which was well attended by those on the dozens of anchored yachts as well as by hotel guests. Jacques hadn't exaggerated when he said Megan would hear many languages and see many different kinds of people. All around her she heard words and phrases in various languages, but the common tongue was English, spoken with an intriguing variety of accents.

As the music provided by a native band grew louder and louder, the steel drums ringing out a lively brand of calypso with a throbbing African undertone, young deck hands with long hair and untrimmed beards mingled with millionaire owners of fabulous yachts and vacationing executives and their wives and daughters and girlfriends. Conversation was drowned out by the compulsive rhythm, and everyone danced with everyone else.

Megan whirled from one partner to the next, finding herself the recipient of more than one good-natured proposition to which she found it impossible to take offense. She was in the midst of explaining to a blue-eyed, blond young Viking that she was not free to join him and his friends for the remainder of the winter even if they were headed for Trinidad when Case appeared at her side, looking for all the world like a disapproving husband. When the young man gave him a cautious glance and quickly faded away into the gyrating crowd, Megan threw back her head and laughed with pure exhilaration.

"What a great shot to my thirty-two-year-old ego!" she exclaimed gaily. "He must be all of twenty-two, and he wants me to sail off into the sunset with him!"

Noticing that Case didn't look in the least amused, it occurred to her that he hadn't been free to enjoy himself this evening as she had. He'd been busy getting shots of Marcelle and capturing the spirit of the Jump-Up on camera.

"How did it go?" she asked with a tinge of apology.

"All right," he replied briefly, taking her arm and leading her out of the crowd. Megan went along with him unquestioningly, feeling his tension and guiltily aware that she hadn't given a thought tonight to her own purpose for being there at the Jump-Up. She had simply thrown herself wholeheartedly into having a good time, trusting blindly in her ability to bring everything together when she actually got down to the task of writing the feature. Shrugging aside her sense of having been remiss, she sought to lighten the seriousness of his mood.

"This sounds like an absolutely fabulous place to vacation," she ventured cheerfully. "One of the guests was telling me that the cottages are all spaced far apart for privacy, each one with its own great view. There aren't any telephones in any of them.

When someone wants room service, he or she just raises a flag over the roof and a hotel employee arrives in minutes driving one of those little mini-moke vehicles to take the order. Doesn't that sound delightful?"

Case grunted noncommittally.

"You can have all your meals in your own cottage if you want to," Megan breezed on, hearing the faintly dogged tone in her voice at his lack of response. "Or you can go to the dining room. The food is supposed to be superb."

They had been walking parallel to the curving shoreline on a grassy strip between the sand and a paved pathway. The sound of the steel band was in the background, growing dimmer. Megan was aware of the night breeze and the tangy freshness of the sea with now and then a tantalizing whiff of tropical flowers. The night was simply too wonderful for conflict or unhappiness.

"Case, can't you just unwind and enjoy a little of this?" she implored wistfully. He had dropped her arm earlier and now she caught up his hand in hers. He didn't jerk it free, but he might as well have. Resistance pulsed from his hard, tensed flesh into hers.

"Believe me, I would if I could," he bit out so harshly that she flinched and then slowly let go of his hand. "It's not easy to kick up my heels when I can't think of much else but last night. Just what was that all about anyway—if you can stop enjoying yourself long enough to fill me in?"

Megan bristled in instinctive reaction to his abrasive tone and the cutting edge of accusation. It was difficult not to go immediately on the defensive when questioned in that manner, but she told herself sternly she would not lose her temper and become embroiled in another bitter argument with him.

"What do you think it was all about?" she asked carefully. "I should have thought it was obvious."

Case jammed his hands into the pockets of his trousers and willed the knotted muscles and tangled nerves to relax. Damn! He hadn't meant to attack her like that. It wasn't her fault he'd been through hell tonight trying to get some decent shots in all that bedlam. And Marcelle hadn't cooperated worth a damn. He didn't know what had happened between her and Yvette today, but something must have. And then when he was finally through, he'd come upon Meg flirting with that Nordic Romeo and been jealous as hell he hadn't been having a good time with her himself. Added to all that, he'd been thinking about last night the whole livelong day, trying to figure out if what had happened would bring about any change for the better.

"I don't know," he said heavily when he trusted himself to speak in a more civil tone. "Maybe to prove there's nothing wrong with me. Maybe to ease your guilt if you thought you might be responsible—" Case fought unsuccessfully to keep back the last and the worst of his suspicions, but it came bursting out, raw and bitter. *"Maybe you just wanted to see if I was still putty in your hands."* He held his breath, hoping she would refute *all* those reasons.

"Is that *all?*" Megan demanded, her voice cracking on the last word, incredulity fast giving way to indignation. "You really have a very high opinion of me these days, don't you, Case? I'm either a sex therapist or some power hungry bitch! Well, maybe I did want to prove there's nothing wrong with you, and maybe I do feel bad about the hell we've both been through the last two years, but didn't it at least *occur* to you that I might have gone into your stateroom last night because *I* wanted to make love with *you*—for *me!*" Megan gulped in a breath of air and made an abortive effort to cut off the tirade. But she was too far gone to stop. Her redhead's temper had run away with her again.

"Is that so hard for you to believe?" she blazed angrily. "Why is it that a woman is not ever supposed to do anything just for herself? Why does she always have to be doing whatever she does for her children or her husband or her parents or—or . . ." Megan floundered, too outraged for a long moment to be able to think clearly. ". . . her in-laws!" she finally managed to choke out.

"Okay, *okay*," Case soothed. "You've made your point."

Megan could have sworn he sounded almost pleased, and her puzzlement over the reason for that reaction helped to dissipate the hot spurt of temper. Something vaguely hesitant in his manner as he ran one hand through his hair warned her he hadn't finished saying everything yet. She braced herself.

"Is this the kind of thing you make a habit of now?" he asked with elaborate casualness.

"What 'kind of thing'?" Megan countered, puzzled. He couldn't mean losing her temper. He knew she'd always done that.

"You know," Case answered evasively. "Going to bed with a man because you want to."

Megan gasped, her shock rendering her speechless momentarily. She felt as though he had just slapped her hard across the face and as soon as the numbness was gone, it would hurt like hell.

"Of all the *nerve*, Case Ballantine," she said slowly. "Here you've admitted to me right out in the open that you've tried to have affairs with other women, and you want to know if *I* sleep around. Well, I just wish I could honestly say *yes!*" Megan gritted her teeth together and took a deep breath to calm herself before she was off on another rampage. "For your information, I don't. If you'd use your common sense, you'd know there isn't much of an opportunity even for a normal social life commuting into the city and having to get home every night and take care of two children who are certainly old enough to notice if their mother had overnight male company and who would—I'm sure—pass that information along to you!"

Megan was suddenly swept by a deep and unexpected flood of homesickness. She felt terribly alone and battered and far away from all that was familiar.

"I need to call home and check on the kids," she said in a small, miserable little voice. "It's too late tonight, though, isn't it?"

Case felt all his resistance to her cave in under his feet and didn't bother to try to summon it again. He could maintain a level of self-protection when she was defiant, but not when she called up in him this fierce tenderness and urge to protect her.

"I'm afraid it is," he conceded gruffly. "I'll talk to the hotel manager tomorrow and arrange to use the phone in the office tomorrow afternoon. We can call about the time the kids should be getting in from school. Ready to go back to the Jump-Up now?"

But Megan found the idea totally unappealing. Her mood had changed. She knew she wouldn't be able to plunge back into the noisy fun.

Chapter Eight

"I'm a little tired," she said quietly. "I think I'll just go back to the boat if someone will take me. But you stay. You didn't get a chance to enjoy yourself earlier."

Case made no effort to dissuade her. They walked back toward the music and the babble of voices and laughter, and when they came to the crowd, skirted its edges.

"Wait here," Case bade at the point where a long wooden pier connected with the land. All along the pier dinghies and inflatable boats were tied up three and four deep. "I'll find somebody to take us back to the yacht," he added.

Megan didn't argue. If he wanted to leave the Jump-Up, that was his prerogative, she told herself tiredly. He could return to the boat and retire to his private stateroom without any fear that *she* would intrude uninvited tonight. His interrogation had left her feeling anything but good about herself in spite of the righteous fury of her self-defense. To have one's spontaneous actions subjected to such suspicion somehow took the joy out of life.

Case returned in about five minutes with a crew member from the schooner, who took them out to *l'Esprit* in the tender. This time when they had gone aboard, there was no fumbling with the key as Case unlocked the main hatch. Megan made her descent down the companionway stairs ahead of him and spoke a restrained "Good night" before entering her stateroom without waiting to give him a chance to detain her.

After she had undressed and stretched out on her bunk, she lay there listening to the slap of the water against the hull and the sound of the wind whistling through the wire rigging. She could feel the boat sway and jerk against the anchor rode. From the shore came the muted sound of the Jump-Up, but the distant revelry somehow only deepened her sense of isolation and loneliness. In vain she tried to resurrect some vestige of excitement in her present situation, but instead she found herself worrying about the deadline she faced.

It was so crucial to her future with Dee Gardner's fashion magazine that Megan do an outstanding job of the feature she was here in the Caribbean to do.

Dee had made it plain this assignment was a test of Megan's potential. And Megan had started out with the blithe assurance that she *would* more than measure up to the test. Yet so far her mind was a jumble of impressions with no clear-cut slant that would bring the whole thing together. While Case's photographs admittedly were the heart of the feature, Megan would have considerable say in selecting the ones the American fashion magazine would use, and her text had to be snappy.

Sighing, Megan had just flopped over on her side, facing the door, when she heard a noise from the stateroom opposite hers. Case was moving around, obviously not asleep yet either. Megan was struck with a sharp longing to get up and go to him, not to lure him into making love to her against his will as she had the previous night, but just to seek his human companionship. She needed to talk about the self-doubts plaguing her tonight, but he probably wouldn't be interested in listening, not about worries pertaining to her job.

Disconsolate at this realization, Megan flopped on her back again and then raised up quickly on her elbows when she heard the click of Case's door opening and then closing. Holding her breath in suspense, she waited but there came no knock on her own door, no call, no indication whatever that Case might feel the need of her company, too. After an interminable lapse of time, Megan couldn't maintain her silence any longer, despite the dictates of pride.

"Case?" she called out softly.

Instantly her door opened, leaving no doubt that he had been standing in the corridor just outside.

"Can't you sleep either?" he inquired sympathetically from the open doorway. "What's wrong? You're not worrying about the kids?"

His voice washed over her like a balm to her troubled spirit. Megan felt herself relaxing and rested her head back on the pillow as he came closer when she didn't answer at once.

"I'm sure they're okay," he reassured, sitting down on the edge of her bunk without touching her.

"It's not worrying about the kids that is keeping me awake," Megan admitted with reluctant candor, not wanting to lose the comfort of his presence. "It's this damned writing assignment."

She could sense him tightening in instinctive resistance and continued hurriedly before he could get up and leave.

"Case, it's so *important* for me to do well with this feature, and so far I don't have a single idea about what angle I should take. I was so sure starting out that I'd be able to handle this—and handle it *well*—I don't know what's wrong! I'm beginning to doubt myself . . ." Megan sighed as she let her voice drift off. It wasn't easy admitting these feelings to Case, knowing how unsympathetic he would be.

"You must have *some* ideas by now." Case's grudging tone made it clear the subject wasn't one he was eager to discuss.

"No, I don't," Megan insisted worriedly. "The whole premise for the feature is an idyllic cruise in a remote part of the world that has been relatively untouched by modern man's technology and so-called progress. Isn't that right?" she put in rhetorically and then didn't wait for him to answer. "The Grenadines are certainly the perfect choice. They're so beautiful I find myself thinking the Garden of Eden must have been something like this . . ."

"Yes," Case prompted when she didn't continue. He had distracted her by shifting his position slightly so that his hip rested against her bare thigh. The feel of soft cotton knit told Megan he was wearing knit briefs. She wondered if he was wearing anything else and disciplined her hands not to reach out and touch him to find out.

"Well, Marcelle looks so conspicuously *phony* in this setting. I mean, there she is in sophisticated designer outfits standing out like a sore thumb against a simple, utterly natural background. All around her are people dressed for comfort and barefoot as often as not. Do you see what I mean at all?" she implored.

"Sure. Move over."

Surprised at the matter-of-fact order, Megan obeyed him instantly, scooting further to the inside of her bunk. Case stretched out beside her, the touch of his hard shoulder against hers telling her his upper torso was bare.

"What you're saying is unquestionably true," Case said thoughtfully, for all the world as if there were nothing unusual about the two of them having this discussion in her bunk. "Marcelle definitely doesn't fit into this setting, and especially not in high fashion garbs. But authenticity has nothing to do with fashion journalism in general. You and I and Cecile are not dealing with reality in this assignment; we're dealing with fantasy. We're producing a slick product for the magazine readers—giving them an imaginative experience, not any statement of truth.''

Megan was so fascinated that she raised up on one elbow, turning sideways toward him. "Go on," she urged.

"What I've been doing," Case continued, "is not down-playing the element of artificiality but rather exaggerating it." He hesitated briefly. "It's not my place to tell you how to do your job, but you'll have to work around my photographs. How would it work to present Marcelle as a modern-day Eve returning to the Garden of Eden? You know, really emphasize the fantasy."

"It would work," Megan said wonderingly, enthusiasm and relief flooding through her as she considered his somewhat reluctant suggestion and felt as though all the pieces in a kaleidoscope had suddenly shifted into place, forming a splendid pattern. "It would work!" she said again, her voice jubilant. "Oh, Case! Thank you! Thank you a million!" Without stopping to think, Megan hugged him, in spite of the fact she wasn't wearing a stitch of clothes.

Case's arms closed immediately around her. With her cheek nestled in the furry warmness of his chest, she lay there contentedly.

"I feel so *relieved*," she breathed happily. "I wish I could return the favor and help you the way you've helped me—but then you don't ever need my help, do you?" she added ruefully. "You're so good at what you do." He was silent, the palm of his hand stroking gently across her shoulders. Megan was struck by a sudden thought that made her raise up.

"Do you realize you've never shared your work with me like this before?" she demanded. "You always shut me out of that part of your life, Case."

As soon as the words were out, she wished she hadn't sounded quite so accusing. And then when Case took his arms from around her and pushed her gently aside, she could have cut out her tongue for having spoiled the wonderful harmony between them.

"Case, I'm sorry," she apologized swiftly. "I didn't mean to sound so bitchy—"

"I never thought of it as shutting you out," Case interrupted stiffly, getting up and sitting on the edge of the bunk. "I just never wanted to bring my work home with me. It was a relief to get away from it a while." Megan bit her lip during a silence she didn't dare break for fear of saying something else wrong. "Maybe I was wrong," Case continued in the same proud, careful tone. "Maybe I've been wrong about a lot of things. If I've been able to help you by giving my own approach to this assignment, well, I'm glad. I know the job's important to you."

Megan's joy had faded as she listened to his voice push her farther and farther away. For a moment they had been so close sharing their common work here in the Caribbean. Why couldn't he enjoy that the way she did?

Case got up and walked over to the door.

"Maybe you'll be able to sleep now that your mind's been put at ease," he suggested and waited for her answer.

Megan fought her pride which reminded her she had been the one to make the overtures the previous night, only to find herself the object of suspicion for her boldness.

"I'm not sleepy," she said simply, keeping the admission carefully devoid of any hint of wheedling.

"Me either."

Megan's whole being willed him to stay, but she bit down hard on her bottom lip to keep back the words of pleading. It was his turn to make a move.

When he came back to the bunk and lay down next to her, she moved into his arms without any trace of reticence, fitting the warm curves of her body to the harder angles and planes of his. At first they caressed each other lightly, exploring, awakening the flames of sexual arousal and feeding them with increasing intimacy.

Megan lay back with a willing languor when Case pushed her away from him and raised up over her, his lips and the soft bristle of his beard wreaking sensual devastation as he nuzzled the curve of her neck and worked his way slowly downward to her eager breasts. Attending to each nipple in turn, he teased them with his tongue and nipped them between his teeth, arousing circles of pleasure that spread through her body in warm pulses, bringing delight and the hunger for more sensation. Megan sighed aloud as she smoothed the palms of her hands across the muscular breadth of his shoulders, then raked him lightly with her nails, setting off a tremor and triggering a sudden new urgency in his caresses.

Sliding down toward the foot of her bunk, Case trailed his lips downward from her breasts to the indentation in her flat abdomen. His hands shaped the narrowness of her waist and curved over her hips down to the supple roundness of her thighs and then slid slowly and deliberately upward again, back to her waist. Megan drew in her breath audibly and let her thighs relax apart, as though willing the wayward hands to come back and attend to the insistent throb in her lower pelvis. Instead he planted little kisses from her abdomen to the sensitive insides of her thighs, taking his time and driving her to a mindless distraction. At the first flickering contact of his warm, rough tongue's invasion of her most private of places, Megan groaned his name aloud and lifted her hips.

It seemed to her as he flicked and probed with his tongue and aggravated the sharp urgency centered between her thighs that all the sensation of the universe was momentarily concentrated there. For the moment nothing else mattered or existed except for the exquisite torture he was administering. The shattering paroxysm brought a cry from her lips, and afterward she lay for seconds limp and utterly spent. Her hands reached down and caressed his head gently to express her gratitude as he kissed the insides of her thighs and brushed his lips against each hip, across the flatness of her stomach, and finally around the fullness of each breast before he stretched out next to her again. Megan felt as though he had paid fervent homage to her woman's body and savored the essence of its shape and resilient softness. He had made her feel beautiful and cherished.

Wishing to give him the same total pleasure he had given her, Megan raised up beside him and kissed him on the mouth, tasting the salty tang of his lips and tongue. Then she lowered her face to his chest, nuzzling her lips into the matted warmth while her hands reached lower to tug at the elastic waist of his briefs. He raised his hips and helped her strip the briefs off, but he was not content to lie quiescent and allow her to attend to his pleasure.

Taking her hand he pressed it hard against his engorged maleness, groaning as she took him in her hand with a familiar skill, delighting in the intimacy of the contact. But Case felt the hot urgency rising too fast, and he pulled away from her, tremors of passion rippling through him as he pressed Megan back on the bunk and positioned himself between her legs, entering with a thrust so deep it took her breath away.

Before she could recover, he was moving inside her, again and again, thrilling her with the power and intensity of his male need, calling forth an answering abandon in her that sent them surging upward on a breathtaking ascent to a cataclysmic release. Case felt as though he had shot straight up to the top of the world just in time for it to explode under his feet and send him shooting out into a crimson-streaked darkness. If possible, he was even more devastated tonight than he had been the previous evening.

"Good Lord," he murmured, taking in a deep breath and mustering all his remaining strength for the daunting task of rolling over. He knew he must weigh a ton to her in his present nerveless condition, and she was such a tiny little thing. "I don't know what you *do* to me . . ." he mumbled. ". . . hundred pounds of TNT . . ."

Megan snuggled close against him, suffused with warm happiness. Later when reality intruded, she knew she would have to come back to earth and face the fact that their transcendent sex changed nothing between them, solved none of their serious problems. They would still be separated by the same essential differences that had torn them apart initially. But for the time being, she couldn't see any further than the circle of Case's arms.

"Meg?"

"Hm?" she mumbled into his chest.

"Would you rather I didn't sleep in here tonight?"

It took a second or two for the question to sink in. Megan pulled slightly away from him to answer in a puzzled tone.

"No—why do you ask? *Oh,*" she added softly, the probable reason suddenly occurring to her. "You mean because I left your stateroom during the night last night?" His silence was confirmation enough. "I didn't come back in here because I didn't want to *sleep* with you, Case," she explained with soft urgency. "I just woke up in the middle of the night and couldn't get back to sleep. I didn't want to disturb you with my tossing and turning. I came back in here and tried—without any success—to come up with some slant on the feature I have to write on this trip."

When he still didn't say anything, Megan wondered if she hadn't convinced him. But his next words, spoken in a resigned tone with a tinge of disappointment told her he had given a perfectly logical interpretation to her explanation that wasn't the whole truth. He thought she hadn't been able to sleep for worrying about the feature when actually her insomnia had resulted initially from a much more serious problem: the split between herself and Case.

"Now that you have a slant, you should be able to sleep," he said quietly.

For a split second Megan was on the verge of correcting his error, but in the past every discussion that touched on the differences separating them had led to a bitter, futile argument. She couldn't take the risk because she wanted more than anything else at the moment for Case to stay right where he was, holding her close against his warm, solid length.

"I'm *sure* I will be able to sleep," she murmured, relaxing again and luxuriating in the wonderful closeness. To make up for her lack of total candor, she added, "I do love you, Case. And to set the record straight, I *haven't* been to bed with any other man the last two years . . . or any other time. You're still my one and only lover . . ."

Case's arms tightened around her so hard the embrace was painful for the space of a few seconds before he relaxed it sufficiently to allow her to breathe.

"You don't know what a heel I feel like," he muttered into her hair. "Do you think you can ever forgive me for—" He broke off, unable to cope with the unpleasantness of putting into words once again what he had already admitted, that he had tried to be unfaithful to her during the past two years while they were apart. "I swear to you I didn't ever really *want* to make love to another woman. I was just so angry at you; in some infantile way, I was trying to punish you."

Megan spoke soothing words of endearment as she reached up with both hands and brought his head to hers for the kiss she meant as a seal of her forgiveness. At first the meeting of their lips was a sweet transaction, with Case mutely asking for understanding and Megan giving it with unstinting generosity of heart and spirit. Then quite without either of them knowing how it had happened, their lips were exchanging messages of a more passionate nature. Case's mouth moved on hers with a resurrected hunger. When he rolled over on his back, bringing her on top of him, Megan could feel the jutting evidence of his quick arousal pressing into her.

She kissed him back, her tongue welcoming the thrusting entry of his inside her mouth and then readily accepting the challenge when his withdrew, tempting her to take on a more aggressive role and come in search. His hands incited the rise of her own passion as he caressed the length of her back, sliding from her shoulders down to her hips and buttocks to squeeze and knead the firmly rounded curves and press her into a more intimate awareness of his burgeoning male need.

When he took her hips in his hands and lifted her lower torso, she read his intention and complied, raising up on her knees to accommodate the union her aroused senses clamored for. The deep entry took away her breath and along with it her strength, a languorous weakness invading all her bones and joints and rendering her momentarily helpless. But his hands clasping her hips urged their movement, and she heeded, slowly, rhythmically, unleashing waves of exquisite pleasure she knew he shared because he spoke her name in a low moan. His hands left her hips and caressed her breasts, cupping and squeezing the roundness, his thumbs worrying the taut nipples and sending out sharp spasms of delight.

It was a temptation for Megan to succumb to the demands of her quickened senses and aroused body. She might have hurried them on to that peak of sensory pleasure ahead of them, but she resisted, and the controlled deliberation of their ascent to climax made it the more shattering when they finally arrived there together. Megan cried out with the jarring force of the explosion inside her and then went limp with the weakness that invaded every cell and defused nerve ending in her body. Case willingly accepted the weight of her slender figure, enclosing her with his arms and holding her spent length on top of him.

Now there was no conversation about who would sleep where the remainder of the night, indeed no conversation about anything at all. Megan fell into a deep relaxed slumber and didn't even know when Case eased her over beside him. Not once during the night did she rouse up with a sense of strangeness that she and Case were sharing a bed after two lonely years of sleeping alone.

The next morning a quiet click awakened her. She opened her eyes just in time to see Case, attired in his briefs, about to ease out of her stateroom door.

"Good morning," she mumbled, arresting his exit.

He glanced back, his face suddenly suffused with tenderness as he regarded her blinking sleepily at him.

"Morning, sleepyhead," he said gruffly, coming back and bending down to plant a quick kiss on her lips. When her arms snaked up around his neck, he removed them with obvious reluctance, but there was firmness in his tone as he dissuaded her from drawing him into any further early-morning intimacy.

"No time for that now, unfortunately. Today's another busy work day."

Megan let out a petulant sigh, but she didn't try to argue with him. "Case?" she called out softly when he had turned away and was headed once again for the stateroom door. "Don't forget you said you'd arrange for a telephone call home this afternoon," she reminded when he hesitated and looked back inquiringly at her.

"I haven't forgotten," he said and left.

Megan didn't get up at once. Stretching languorously, she allowed herself several deeply satisfying minutes during which she recalled the happenings of the previous evening, the marvelous exchange of ideas between herself and Case about their common assignment as well as the sheer glory of their love-making. How could something positive and healing to their relationship *not* arise out of such a meeting of minds and bodies? Suffused with optimism about the future, she got up and set about getting dressed.

It was another golden tropical day, sunlight bathing the lush green vegetation of Petit St. Vincent in brilliance that hurt the unshaded eye. The blue sea was transformed into a huge, glittering sapphire. The trade breezes blew steadily, cooling the sun-heated skin and beguiling the unwary into forgetting about the dangers of dehydration in the hot climate.

The first part of the day Case photographed Marcelle ashore on the cottage premises of an eagerly accommodating guest. The diet-conscious model actually consumed almost none of a sumptuous brunch that was served on the terrace as part of the fiction that she was being entertained by acquaintances vacationing on the island.

At noon the members of the crew were guests of the hotel for lunch, a lavish buffet Megan found she had little appetite to eat. She felt lethargic and tired and looked forward to the midday siesta she was fast learning to be a necessity here in the tropics.

When Case went to his own stateroom upon their return to the yacht, Megan felt no sense of slight. He had exerted himself much more than she had, mentally as well as physically, taking roll after roll of film and getting the most out of his subjects. For the first time she could appreciate his dedication to his work when he was on an assignment like this one. He not only gave one hundred percent of himself during actual working hours; he was also careful to keep himself well rested and physically fit for the demands of the job.

As she lay down in her bunk after a quick, cooling shower, Megan mused that it was unfortunate that she had never accompanied Case on an assignment before this one. If she had, things might have been much different. She wouldn't have nursed that little resentment for being deprived of all the excitement and glamour she imagined Case was enjoying without her. She would have seen the intensity he put into his work and understood why he wasn't eager to talk about a trip once it was over and he had returned home. She knew now how much he had needed respite from the total concentration he brought to a job, from the pressures of getting the best from models, from the actual physical rigors, as well.

With her lips parted into a contented half-smile, Megan drifted off to sleep, looking forward to the time when she would be alone with Case that evening. She couldn't wait to tell him this new insight she had gained into his working world and her own misconceptions about it. Surely an admission of the kind she intended to make would open his mind to her own needs. He might at least give consideration to the possibility that her career aspirations didn't diminish her love for him and the children.

Megan's last waking thought was a reminder to

herself that she and Case would be telephoning home later that afternoon. Case had arranged it with the hotel management. They would be talking to their children together, the four of them a family again, even separated as they were by distance. . . .

Chapter Nine

Some hours later Megan understood as she never had before the truth of that old maxim "ignorance is bliss." She would not have slept so soundly had she known what news awaited her.

From the outset the telephone call to Connecticut did not work out as she had drowsily anticipated that it would, as a kind of reestablishment of family solidarity, also a strong hint to the children that their parents were on the road to being back together again. To begin with, Case didn't know if she would prefer to talk with her mother and the two children in private. He approached the matter obliquely so as not to cause either of them awkwardness.

"Why don't I order us a couple of drinks in the lounge while you make the call?" he suggested casually. "Would you tell the kids hello for me and give them my love?"

"Why don't you tell them yourself?" Megan blurted out, flooded with disappointment that Case did not share her state of mind.

"Why, I will—if you don't mind," he said with alacrity.

"Why should I mind?" Megan demanded. "You're their father, after all. They'll want to talk to *you* as much as to me."

She shoved aside a totally illogical uneasiness, refusing to consider for the moment that she might be deluding herself in believing that she and Case were coming closer together on this Caribbean trip. Her first priority was to summon a somewhat dulled enthusiasm for the long-distance exchange. She owed it to her mother and two children to be cheerful and receptive.

"Hello," came her mother's voice, its barely perceptible Irish brogue disconcertingly clear.

Megan knew the instant she heard it that something was wrong, even before Frances O'Riley perceived that her daughter was the caller. When she did reach that realization, she poured out the bad news plaguing her in such a way as to bring the deepest terror to Megan's breast.

"Megan, darling, it's you! Thank God! It must be the will of the good Lord that you called! I've been half out of my mind not knowing whether I should get word to you. But I didn't want to spoil your wonderful trip when there's nothing you can *do* way down there—it's your poor little Danny—"

Megan jerked the receiver away from her ear, the white-knuckled hand holding it trembling with her terrible fear. Her eyes, wide and frightened in a chalk-white face, sought Case's.

"It's Danny," she whispered. "Oh, Case— something's *happened* to him—"

"*Danny!*" Case ejaculated, grabbing the phone from her rigid grip. "Frances, what's wrong with Danny?" he barked sternly into the receiver. "Just calm down and tell me everything." As he listened his tense expression underwent immediate relief and he covered the mouthpiece to erase the horror in Megan's white face. "Meg, Danny's all right. He just has a broken leg, that's all."

Megan went limp with the incredible relief. Soon afterward she was reaching for the telephone, wanting to hear from her mother all the details now that she knew they wouldn't be more than she could bear.

"Hold on a minute, Frances," Case told his mother-in-law. "Megan wants to talk to you again."

It took some minutes for Megan to satisfy herself that she had all the details from her distraught parent. Danny's school bus had been involved in a serious collision that had resulted in numerous injuries to the children, but fortunately no casualties. Danny had suffered a simple leg fracture that the doctor assured his grandmother would heal without any complications. In the meantime he had to wear the usual cast.

"Let me talk to Kathleen, please, Mother," Megan requested when her mother was about to begin another recap of the whole series of events. Twelve-year-old Kathleen gave a much more lucid and unemotional account of the accident and also inadvertently gave Megan an insight into the reason her mother was in such a highly emotional state. Danny apparently wasn't taking his accident well at all.

"Everybody—even the *doctor*—has tried to tell Danny his leg will be okay," Kathleen explained in an exasperated tone. "But from the way he's acting, you'd think he has to have it *amputated*. Maybe *you* can reason with him, Mother. You know he likes you better than anybody else. Was Grandma talking to Daddy?" she inquired eagerly in a quick change of subjects. "Can I talk to him?"

"Sure, honey, in a little bit," Megan promised. "First, I want to talk to your brother. Put him on, will you, please?"

Inside she was torn apart with the frustration of her situation. If only she could close her eyes, breathe a wish, and open them to find herself at home, talking to her little son in person. Kathleen was right when she said Danny depended on his mother more than anyone else. He had always been close to her, confiding in her thoughts he wouldn't tell his sister or even his father. Right now Megan knew she could understand him and comfort him better than anyone else would be able to do. Talking to him on the telephone was anything but satisfactory, but it was the best she could do at the moment.

"How are you, honey?" she asked as brightly as

she could manage after he had said a somewhat subdued hello. In childlike fashion he wasted no time getting right to the heart of his fears.

"Mom, when I get well, do you think I'll be able to run and . . . you know, *everything* . . ." he asked worriedly.

Megan understood at once what he was really asking. His ineffectual effort at camouflage was her total undoing. She managed to keep her tears back just long enough to say, "Honey, I'm *sure* your leg won't keep you from playing basketball. Now, here's your father. He wants to talk to you—"

She thrust the receiver at Case as though it were a baton being handed to a fresher, stronger runner in a relay race. The tears running down her face welled up out of an overwhelming sense of thanksgiving. She had glimpsed a black pit of sorrow real to any parent during those seconds she had feared the worst about Danny. Now she felt as though she had been spared and was deeply grateful.

Listening to Case's low, quiet voice as he conversed with his son and then with the daughter who thought he was the most special person on earth, Megan breathed a fervent prayer of thanks that Case had been right beside her today. She didn't even care to think what it would have been like for her without his strength and solidity.

When Case covered the mouthpiece of the receiver with his hand and asked if she would like to get back on the phone again with her mother, Megan shook her head, knowing she would learn nothing new to help her with the difficult decision she had to make now: Should she stay here and finish the assignment or should she go home and look after Danny?

"Case, I don't know what to *do!*" she said as soon as he had hung up.

Case shrugged, understanding very well her deep sense of helplessness. For him this was not a new experience to telephone home and learn bad news that made him wish he were there and able to help.

"There's nothing really you *can* do," he replied sympathetically. "Nothing either of us can do until we get back."

Megan stared at him, unbelievingly at first and then resentfully as it dawned on her he hadn't understood the nature of her indecision at all. He was simply assuming that she would stay and finish out the assignment!

"But Danny needs me now." The note of accusation in the statement questioned whether he was really thinking as a father should think in these circumstances.

"Of course, he needs you," Case replied a little impatiently. "He always needs you, with or without a broken leg that's not going to heal any faster whether you're there with him or not."

Megan bit her lip, knowing that Case was saying aloud what one part of herself knew to be true, the part of her that wasn't a mother.

"Think of the trauma he's been through. Poor baby must have been so *scared* . . . and he must have had a lot of *pain* . . ." Megan's eyes were haunted with all she imagined that her young son had suffered while she was miles away and totally oblivious to his suffering.

Case could think of no suitable reply since what she envisioned was undoubtedly true. He accompanied her in silence outside to the waiting mini-moke that would take them from the hotel office to the pier where the *l'Esprit* dinghy was tied up. When he tried several times during the ride to reassure her only to have her snap at him in clipped monosyllables, he lost some of his patience.

"Look, Meg, there's no point in brooding about what you can't change. Believe me, I understand the way you're feeling now. Think of all the times I've called home from God knows where and found you in the middle of some crisis or getting over one that had just happened. How do you think *I* felt when I found out Kathleen was in the hospital with acute appendicitis, for example? Or even that Danny's pet chicken had gotten out on the street and been killed by a passing car?" Case could see that his effort at lightness hadn't been successful at all. "It's a helpless feeling, but there's just nothing you can do."

"But you're not Danny's *mother!*" Megan blurted out. "You don't understand!" Her reproachful eyes met the sharp scrutiny in his.

"What is it you want to do, Meg?" Case made his voice carefully toneless. It had just dawned on him what Megan had wanted from him all along and why she was so resentful. She wanted him to *tell* her she should go home to Danny.

"I *want* to go home and look after Danny!" Megan cried out impatiently. "That's what my gut instinct tells me to do! But I have a responsibility to Dee and the magazine to stay here and carry out this assignment. If I don't, Dee will never understand.

You know darned well she won't! I can't be in two places at the same time, Case! I can't be two people!"

Case found himself up against one of the greatest foes of his lifetime as he battled with his own gut instinct, which had always made him want to smooth things out for Megan, make things easier for her. She had all but begged him to tell her what to do. But things weren't really that simple. She had to realize that the choice she had made two years ago led inevitably to the place where she stood now, torn with indecision. She had chosen a career over home and family when she decided working was more important to her than being his wife and homemaker. Didn't she realize she would have to make choices like this one she faced now over and over with one role or the other always losing out?

"You're right, Meg," Case agreed soberly. "You can't be two people in two different places at the same time."

Megan was quite sure she had never been more alone in her life as she heard Case agree with her in that noncommittal manner. Her brief flash of resentment at him was short-lived as honesty compelled her to admit he was right in forcing her to make her own decision, especially considering the possible effects it could have upon her career.

When the mini-moke braked to a stop near the pier, Megan climbed out in a daze and stood waiting while Case thanked the smiling young driver and tipped him. When the small, open vehicle had driven away, Megan walked several steps beside Case along the pier and then stopped.

"Wait!" she pleaded, meeting the questioning of Case's gaze with eyes that implored him to understand. "I've got to think this through *now*, don't you see? If I'm going to fly back to the States right away, I should make travel arrangements."

Case steeled himself not to show any expression at all as a wild hope was born in his breast.

"We're not without communication on the yacht," he pointed out, feeling the need to say something without influencing her one way or the other. "There's the marine radio, remember."

Megan nodded her head absently and then took slow steps along the pier in the direction of the dinghy, talking as she went.

"If I leave right in the middle of this assignment, there's no doubt that Dee Gardner will write me off as a hysterical mother. It would be the end of my career with her magazine, and not only that, the word would get around to the other editors. After all, Danny isn't seriously ill. He just has a broken leg . . ." Megan's words of common sense had the opposite effect of what she had intended, intensifying the ache of frustration inside her rather than assuaging it. "But I still wish I were there at home with him! I could make sure he was comfortable and fix him the special meals I know he likes and— oh, Case, this is awful!" she cried out in an anguished tone that cut right through him. "I *hate* it!"

Their last few steps had brought them abreast of the place where the dinghy was tied up. Case made no effort to bend over and take the painter off the cleat. He was too busy fighting a losing battle with himself and figuring out a way he could save Megan from her dilemma.

"Look," he said abruptly. "We can *both* leave immediately and go back to the States. I'll tell Dee Gardner it was *my* decision. That way she won't hold you responsible."

"But you can't do that!" Megan's instant rejection of his suggestion was plainly horrified. "Think of what it would do to *your* reputation, which is more important than mine will ever be! It would be different if Danny were seriously ill, but . . ." Megan's own words began to sink into her consciousness, bringing with them the sudden awareness of what she should do. She finished the argument she had been making, her tone resigned. "He only has a simple fracture."

Her eyes met his for a long, somber moment, communicating the message she didn't have to speak aloud: Megan would stay and complete the assignment. She was, after all, a professional with responsibilities to others, just as Case was. She should operate by the same rules that he did.

The decision brought with it a sense of compromise that Megan hadn't been prepared for. Before now she had been so confident she could satisfy the demands of being both a career woman and a wife and mother, without any serious conflicts of interest. She saw now that the emotional tug-of-war she had just been through was inevitable and would happen again from time to time. Undoubtedly the strain she felt would leave marks, whether they were visible or not. All of which meant that in a way, Case had been right all along, hadn't he?

Case didn't see the dispirited droop of Megan's shoulders as she faced up to the unpleasant by-products of her decision. With the first awareness that she was going to stay, he was hit by a pain deep in his gut, the kind that made him want to double over. He bent and untied the painter, taking his time about it and welcoming the numbness that gradually spread through him. That brief hope that had flared up when he realized Megan was actually considering going home at once to Danny was dead now. And all the rest of him felt dead, too. In its own way, feeling nothing was a great relief.

He didn't disapprove of Megan's decision on logical or moral grounds, but her weighing of priorities had resulted in her doing what was best for her career. Case knew all too well the price of success. He had paid it himself in time and energy—and now it meant nothing to him.

Megan was so emotionally drained that she didn't try to draw Case into conversation during the few minutes it took to get down into the dinghy and motor out to the yacht floating gracefully at anchor, rays of afternoon sun adding a deeper luster to the royal-blue hull. She did note Case's remoteness, but interpreted it as his own way of coping with the sobering news of the telephone conversation. She wondered if, like herself, he was more keenly aware of all the danger life held for one's children. In her mind, Kathleen and Danny were more vulnerable and more dear to her than they had ever been before. In deciding not to go home at once, she felt more poignantly the ache of being a mother.

Everyone, including Jacques and Alina, dined

aboard the schooner that night. Megan found herself with no opportunity to talk to Case alone, a situation she found most frustrating since she needed to talk about the insight she'd gained that day into the difficulties of managing a career and home responsibilities. She wanted to ask Case if through the years of being husband, father, and provider, he had ever had to deal with the same sense of conflict and compromise that she was feeling.

There was no chance of a private conversation with him later, after the two of them along with Jacques and Alina had returned to *l'Esprit*. When Jacques suggested a nightcap, Case refused immediately.

"Not for me. It's been a long day. If the rest of you will excuse me, I think I'll say good night and turn in." With a glance that took in Megan but did not single her out or impart a personal message, he retired to his stateroom.

Megan smarted with a sense of rebuff she tried to hide from the French couple. That night she lay awake long after she was sure all the rest of the world must be sleeping. In addition to her emotional fatigue and the unrest arising out of her own inner questioning, she was deeply hurt that Case had acted toward her as he had this evening. She might have been some stranger he hardly knew. If he cared for her, wouldn't he be offering her his support at a time when he surely must know she needed it? She hadn't tried to hide from him how painful that decision had been for her this afternoon.

The following day it became dismayingly clear to Megan that whatever was wrong with Case hadn't been cured by a night's sleep. He remained utterly detached in his attitude toward her and everyone else, as well.

On the passage from Petit St. Vincent to the next island, Carriacou, he and Megan sailed aboard the schooner, an experience Megan had eagerly looked forward to but found robbed of much of its expected pleasure now. Case worked as hard as ever, photographing Marcelle in various poses of leisure, but today he said nothing that wasn't required to get the job done. By the time they had arrived at the anchorage off Carriacou, Cecile and Yvette were giving him curious looks. At the first opportunity Cecile even questioned Megan tactfully, mentioning that she hoped Case wasn't coming down with a tropical illness at this stage in the cruise.

"He's had some upsetting news from home," Megan said vaguely, deciding it would be best to give the other woman some explanation to allay her concern without going into revealing details. "Nothing really serious, though. I wouldn't mention it to him, if I were you."

Cecile raised her fine, penciled eyebrows thoughtfully. It was obvious to Megan that the French writer wanted to say more.

"Have you known Case long?" she asked casually, as though the matter were only of trivial interest.

"Thirteen years," Megan replied in a friendly manner. Some curiosity to see where the conversation would lead made her not discourage the other woman from pursuing it.

"That long." The eyebrows arched upward again, higher this time. The quick smile was openly apologetic. "Forgive my woman's curiosity, Megan. It is just that Case has had for so many years the reputation for being the devoted family man. He was never open to even a harmless little flirtation."

Megan's whole face lighted with such gladness that Cecile was plainly bemused. Without even stopping to think about the consequences of such a confidence, Megan said softly, "Case is my husband, Cecile. The reason we haven't said anything about it to anyone is that we've been separated the past two years."

The revelation took Cecile by surprise, but she adjusted to it quickly. Her eyebrows climbed up her narrow forehead, lowered, and then climbed again as her agile mind leaped on to other questions.

"I am frankly amazed," she declared gaily. "Not once have I ever heard that Case Ballantine was married to a fashion journalist."

"That was the problem. He didn't want to be married to one—or to any woman with a career," Megan heard herself explaining. "Case is one of those old-fashioned men who don't want their wives to work." It was clear from her tone that she expected Cecile to have little sympathy for such a point of view.

Cecile glanced past Megan toward the bow of the schooner where Case had gone a few minutes earlier to sit by himself and drink a bottle of beer. He sat looking out at the green hillsides of the island of Carriacou, apparently deeply absorbed in thought.

"It is also very old-fashioned to be faithful to one's wife, is it not?" Cecile asked unexpectedly.

Megan was taken aback by the remark she hadn't

expected from a successful careerwoman like Cecile, a woman of sophistication and polish.

"Are you married, Cecile?" Megan asked impulsively.

The Frenchwoman's smile was faintly ironic.

"Not at the present time. But I have been married —three times, as a matter of fact. And never to an 'old-fashioned' man like Case Ballantine." Her tone implied that she had not been so fortunate, and if she had, she would not be so foolish as to let him go.

"Please don't mention what I've told you, Cecile." Megan's request was absentminded, her attention focused on Case up at the bow of the schooner.

"But of course." Cecile agreed without any hesitation, her slight shrug implying the matter was forgotten already.

The small exchange gave Megan the shot of courage she needed to face Case head on and ask him what was the matter. As she headed toward him along the wide side deck she resolved to get to the bottom of the way he was acting toward her, with such coolness, as though the intimacies they had shared on this trip were all a figment of her imagination.

Case must have been alerted to her approach somehow because he looked around before she had covered more than half the distance between them. Immediately he stood up and started toward her.

Megan stopped. "But I was coming to sit a minute with you," she said in a mildly affronted tone. "I need to talk to you, Case."

He didn't answer until he had reached her.

"I'm not much in the mood for talking, Meg," he

said thoughtfully, looking at her in much the same distant way he had been gazing out at the tropical landscape.

"But, Case, what's *wrong?*" Megan's sense of urgency overrode her pride. "Are you worried about Danny? Is it something to do with this assignment that you haven't told me? You've been acting so strange ever since yesterday afternoon . . ." Her voice trailed off as she pinpointed the exact beginning of his withdrawn behavior. It had been right after she had decided to stay and finish her assignment rather than rush home to Danny. She'd noticed Case's silence but had assumed he was going through the emotional aftermath of fear and worry, as she herself was doing.

"Case, are you acting this way because you're disappointed that I didn't go home to Danny?" Her eyes searched his face for an answer, but if her question had touched a sensitive place, it didn't show.

Case took in a deep breath and expelled it, rubbing the fingers of one hand over his chin in a familiar motion that usually indicated impatience. His voice, though, wasn't impatient. Its resigned weariness sent a wave of uneasiness through Megan.

"Look, Meg, I don't want to talk about it now. Or about anything else, for that matter. Just leave me alone, *please.* I have a lot of thinking to do."

Megan felt the same kind of panic she might have felt if Case had just fallen overboard and his stunned body was floating away, out of her reach. It seemed of the greatest necessity that she penetrate his numb calmness and make contact with him.

"But we've *got* to talk, Case!" she insisted desperately. "There's so much we have to discuss . . ."

She might have been talking to herself. Case was looking past her, waiting politely for her to finish. Megan instinctively switched to another tactic.

"I don't know what kind of game you're playing with me, Case Ballantine," she said with tight-lipped dignity. "But I gave you every chance yesterday afternoon to tell me what you thought I should do. You wouldn't say the first word. Now you needn't act as though I'm some kind of negligent mother because I stayed to finish this job. You said yourself Danny wasn't in serious condition."

Case's features softened almost imperceptibly as he noted the way she swallowed and blinked her lashes furiously to hold back the tears.

"Please believe me, Meg. I'm not trying to put any kind of guilt trip on you for staying and doing your job, the same way I'm doing."

The words spoken in a kind tone had the opposite effect of reassurance. Megan wished he had reacted to her indignation with some show of strong emotion, even anger or accusation. This totally calm, impassive Case was a stranger to her, not the man she knew so well who was capable of great passion and tenderness as well as equally strong fury and wrongheadedness. For the first time she could remember, Meg had the distinctly disturbing feeling that nothing she could do or say right now would *touch* Case. He was totally impervious to her, like someone anesthetized on the inside.

"Case, something *is* wrong with you," she whispered, looking at him with dismayed, pleading eyes.

Her hand reached out to grasp his arm as if trying to establish some contact. "You're acting like a *zombie*. Everyone's noticed. Cecile even asked me if you weren't feeling well."

Case frowned slightly as he dropped his eyes to the small rigid fingers clutching him. Their tremor pulsed into his hard flesh and stirred something deep inside him. He noted the involuntary pang with something like irritation and made himself resist the sudden urge to shake off her hand. Would she always have the power to move him, even if he decided to exorcise her from his life?

"I'm all right, Meg, honestly." The effort at lightness came at a high price, but her words had made him realize he couldn't just retire into his own thoughts, no matter how much he might need to do that right now. If he didn't summon the show of normalcy, he would draw more unwanted attention and questions. "I'm just tired, that's all. Maybe it's the heat." He patted the hand gripping his arm before he gently but firmly dislodged it and eased past her, continuing along the deck toward the stern. "I thought I'd go back to the other boat now and catch a nap," he called over his shoulder. "How about you?"

"Oh. I guess so," Megan said uncertainly and trailed along behind him since there seemed nothing else to do. She was deeply dissatisfied with the exchange but baffled as to how to make any inroads into that strange calmness he claimed was fatigue. In his present mood, how could she talk about all the thoughts pressing on her mind?

That evening Case was more like himself, appearing relaxed and rested and joining in the conversation enough not to cause raised eyebrows. But the dismay inside Megan grew into something closer to fear as she noted the continued absence of any special intimacy in Case's voice or his eyes when he spoke to her. She might have been just another of his professional associates on this trip, like Cecile or Marcelle or even the lackluster young hairdresser, René.

Over and over Megan pondered the change in Case. The only explanation for it seemed to be her decision not to fly home to Danny after she learned of his injury. But why hadn't Case tried to influence her when she was caught up in the throes of making that decision? Why couldn't he be open and honest with her now and *tell* her what was in his heart and on his mind? Troubled as she was by Case's behavior and her inability to answer these questions, Megan made no further efforts to force his confidence.

At night she would lie awake in her bunk and think of those rapturous times they had made love before the telephone call to Connecticut. The physical closeness had raised such high hopes in her breast. When she thought of Case now, lying just a few feet away from her, desire quickened her body and frustration aroused a familiar ache only he could assuage. But there was no chance now that she would enter his stateroom uninvited, as she had done that other time. First, he would have to give some sign to indicate that she still mattered to him.

Chapter Ten

*M*egan had wandered a little away from the others. As she let her gaze feast on the open marketplace with its colorful array of fruits and vegetables and spices native to Grenada, she drew into her lungs the blend of aromas and felt a stir of exhilaration that came as a pleasant surprise. It reminded her of her initial anticipation when she had looked upon this trip to the Caribbean as a grand adventure, more vacation than the hard work it had turned out to be.

In many ways the trip had been a disappointment, the biggest one being that she and Case seemed farther apart now than they had ever been. But today, her last full day in the Windward Islands, she felt lighter and younger and more optimistic than she had in days. The smile on her lips stayed there for no good reason other than a general sense of well-being.

"Here you are."

Megan turned toward the sound of the voice hailing her and watched Case as he threaded his way through the crowded marketplace, shaking his head in polite refusal to the many offers from native vendors who held out coconuts and mangoes and little handwoven baskets of spices to tempt the stranger.

"Sorry," Megan apologized in a totally unrepentant voice when he had almost reached her. "Isn't this great?" Her sweeping gesture took in the whole marketplace. "You know, I think St. George's is my favorite of all the places we've been!" She held up for his inspection a tiny, crudely woven basket filled with shiny whole nutmegs and pieces of cinnamon resembling heavy brown parchment plus some other spices she couldn't identify. "See what I bought?"

Case eyed the basket with pretended admiration.

"How nice. Something to take home along with your miniature steel drums and carved black coral," he teased. "The local merchants will be sorry to see you go, I'm sure."

The lighthearted sound of his voice and the relaxation so evident in his whole bearing made Megan's optimism swell. This change in Case was one main reason she felt so good today. He was looking and acting more like himself now that the last picture had been snapped earlier in the day. It was as though some heavy burden had been suddenly lifted from his shoulders.

"I can't buy another thing," she admitted cheerfully. "Unless I throw away some of my clothes, that is." She adopted a mock serious expression as though she were giving consideration to the idea and then laughed when Case eyed her skeptically.

"The others want to hire a couple of taxis and tour the island," he informed her. "Interested?"

"I'd *love* to!" Megan replied at once, her spirits not dampened by the fact that she would have to share Case's company with "the others." By now she had accustomed herself to his not choosing to spend time alone with her.

The afternoon passed pleasantly as they were driven over narrow, rutted roads that could hardly qualify as public highways in most parts of the United States. The two taxi drivers, both knowledgeable young men eager to talk about their island to these interested visitors, stopped the cars often and got out to point out various native plants, many bearing fruit Megan found wonderfully exotic. As they climbed higher and higher into the mountains there were breathtaking vistas of the city of St. George's below and the aqua sea spreading out to the horizon.

After a journey through a lush, green rain forest, where the huge plants crowded them on either side of the road and the air was too steamy to breathe, they all got out of the taxis and walked down a forest pathway, accompanied by a flock of native children who chanted poems of welcome and offered flowers to the ladies. At a steep waterfall with a deep, placid pool at its base, young divers scrambled up steep rocks to the top of the waterfall, posed, and then plunged down into the pool below, to emerge and accept the East Caribbean currency they plainly expected to be paid as a reward for their daring. On the way back to the taxis Megan learned somewhat to her disillusionment that the youngster who had regaled her with his poem of welcome to his island and presented her with a flower also expected to be tipped.

"Young to be so mercenary," she murmured to Case, holding out her hand for the change he dug up from his pockets.

"The fruits of tourism," he commented pragmatically.

It was late when they arrived back at the marina where both the *Marie Antoinette* and *l'Esprit* were docked. Megan's head was awhirl with all she had seen that day. She felt herself under the spell of the vivid tropical beauty and the magical atmosphere of Grenada.

"Today has been perfect," she told Case with a soft, happy sigh. "It makes the whole trip worthwhile." She was quiet a moment, wondering if the day had been so special because finally she had been able to enjoy it with Case without the feature hanging over their heads. "I'll always remember the afternoon you taught me to snorkel, too," she added, a wistful expression entering her vivid blue eyes as she recalled the pure enchantment of gazing down into the fascinating underwater world of Horse Shoe Reef. There had been the added pleasure of sharing the experience with Case, who had never been far away from her the whole time. "Sometime I'd like to come back again, when I didn't have to worry about getting a job done," she said whimsically and wondered at the fleeting expression on Case's face. Had he looked guilty?

That evening they all dined at a small restaurant on the waterfront in St. George's. There was no menu, rather a buffet that featured as the main course a whole roasted pig, accompanied by great bowls of salad and side dishes of rice and potatoes. Everyone in their group seemed in high spirits with even the usually taciturn Marcelle showing a rare animation as she pretended to be posing in front of the serving table with the roasted pig.

Munching on her food, Megan thought about the difference between this, the last night the crew would be together, and that first night on Young Island when she had met all of them. So much had happened between then and now. The time elapsed seemed much longer than ten days and yet it had flown past. She hadn't made any close friends among the French people, but there was a sense of camaraderie that came from working together with a common purpose in mind.

"Want to taste the gin and coconut juice?" Case's inquiry broke into her reflections.

Megan wrinkled up her nose in distaste, but she reached for the glass Case held out toward her and took a tiny sip. "No, *thanks!*" she declared with a shudder, handing the glass back to him. "It tastes as bad as I expected it to."

"It is pretty awful, isn't it?" he agreed cheerfully. "Like another glass of wine?" he inquired, glancing at her empty glass.

"No, thanks," she refused contentedly. "We'll be getting up early to leave tomorrow morning, remember. I don't want to start home with a hangover."

As her eyes met his she wondered if he was thinking, as she was, about their first night in the Caribbean. He had spoken essentially the same sentiment, not wanting to drink too much and begin the assignment with a hangover.

"Time has a way of flying by, doesn't it?" she mused and then mocked herself, "Original words of wisdom from Madame Confucius here!"

But Case wasn't smiling. "How right you are," he said gravely. "It goes by damned fast. That's one of the things I've had a chance to think about lately."

Megan wished now she hadn't gotten them off on this philosophical vein. Searching her mind, she came up with a change of subject.

"I heard earlier tonight that Alina is flying back to France with the others. Her mother has taken seriously ill. Did you know that?" When Case nodded, his somber mood not noticeably lightened, she rattled on. "I wonder what Jacques will do for crew without her. They were leaving here and taking the boat back up to St. Lucia to pick up some charter guests."

Case paused a moment as though waiting to get her full attention. "I've offered to stay and help Jacques move the boat up to St. Lucia. I may even stay on longer."

"You're *staying*—" Megan stared at him, letting the news sink in. "But—but you were flying back to New York with me tomorrow . . ."

Thoughts jumbled her brain, bringing nothing but uneasiness. She thought about Case's moodiness the last week, his vague remarks about being tired and needing to think. His fatigue, she knew, was more mental than physical. She didn't want to go off and leave him here alone in his present psychological state.

"Not thinking of just chucking everything, are you?" She tried to make it sound like a joke.

Case saw the shadow of worry darkening her blue eyes and sought to reassure her. "You know me better than that. I'm just taking a much-needed rest from the rat race, that's all." He grinned. "Not that I'll be shipping my cameras home along with the film I've shot for this feature. I want to take a lot of pictures, the kind of pictures that interest *me.*"

Megan did feel a little better. "I just hope you feel guilty staying down here and island hopping while I go back to snow and ice," she remarked accusingly.

Case wished at that second that life had the same possibilities for ignoring reality that one accepted in fiction and cinema. If he were an actor in a movie, he would turn to Megan and urge, "Stay here with me, my love. We'll rediscover the garden together. We'll bask in the golden sun, swim in the blue, clear water, and walk barefoot in the white sand. All the scars in our souls will heal. All the disappointments in ourselves and in others will vanish. Again there will be joy in the moment and happiness in our oneness

of spirit and body." Case felt all the yearning of
these poetic words inside him, but aloud he said to
Megan, "You can stay, too. I'm sure Jacques would
be glad for another hand."

"A *galley* hand," Meg countered ruefully. She
was thinking wistfully of how much she would like to
stay with Case and truly enjoy this paradise with
him, with no Cecile and Marcelle, no feature to
dominate their time and energy. But there was her
job to consider, the children. . . . And he hadn't
really sounded as though he meant the invitation.

"Case, you *will* let me know as soon as you get
back to New York, won't you?" she urged. By then
he should be rested mentally and physically. They
would sit down and talk in depth about her discover-
ies and insights into herself and into their relationship the last week and a half. Perhaps then they
would be able to take some positive steps about
resuming their life together but with a new understanding.

"Sure I will," he assured her lightly. "Now off
with that serious expression. There's a Jump-Up
back at the marina tonight and I don't have to take a
single picture!"

Megan was aware even as she smiled back at Case
that underlying his gaiety was a forced quality. He
was obviously making the effort—for her, she was
sure—to be carefree on this, her last evening in
Grenada and in the Caribbean.

"What are we waiting for?" she demanded.

But this Jump-Up wasn't like the one at Petit St.
Vincent, where they had danced under the open sky

on the grass and the sand with the presence of the sea just yards away. Here they stood in line outside an enclosed area to pay their money and be stamped on the arm. The music blaring out from inside was recorded and amplified, not the pulsing rhythm of a live band. For the most part it was popular rock music from the States.

Megan tried not to permit herself to compare, not to let her mind dwell for more than a second or two on the thought that life is a continuum and every single experience is uniquely different, a once-in-a-lifetime opportunity. She threw herself into the dancing until the adrenaline pumping through her blood vessels made her abandon real. There was no time but the now. This was Grenada. A high fence enclosed the area, but the tropical sky arched high over her head. The music throbbed and swelled, filling every crack and crevice along the ground and then bouncing off and reverberating in her head, in her limbs and torso. Her heart beat in time to the tempo.

One similarity to the Jump-Up in Petit St. Vincent was that she found herself whirled from partner to partner. For the space of several dances, she lost sight of Case. Then the music changed to a slow, throbbing love song. Suddenly he was there, claiming her.

"Thank God!" she gasped, collapsing into his arms and nestling against him as though she'd come home. "I'm not in shape for this," she groaned.

"Looks like you're one of the popular girls at the high school prom," Case teased. "Must be that red hair. It's what first drew my attention." He stroked his hand along the soft line of her hair, thinking that he could feel the fiery color of it.

Megan quickly shoved aside that earlier perception that Case was *trying* too hard. Then the blatantly sexual music claimed all her senses, and she yielded herself to the sensuality of moving with Case in time with it. He held her close so that her breasts were flattened against the hardness of his chest. Her hips and thighs were welded to his, the slow gyration of their movement awakening the first vague aching awareness in her lower torso, an awareness that quickly sharpened and spread, causing her to press even closer to him.

The movement of their bodies together was dancing in its primitive sense, where the elemental spirit of the music calls up an uninhibited response in the flesh, dancers becoming both the music and the dance. Then by common unspoken consent, Case and Megan no longer moved their feet but stood in the same place, swaying and straining against each other. Case ran his hands down her back, pressing the palms and fingers hard into the pliant softness of her flesh and curving around her buttocks. Lifting her up so that her feet no longer touched the ground, he held her against him, the thrust of his hips against hers slow and circular and honestly sexual in time to music that filled all his pores. The hard swollen proof of his need for her was statement enough that they would have to pursue this intense intimacy to its inevitable end.

As the music died away they stood for several

seconds still locked together, Megan with her arms clinging around his neck and Case with his hands buried in the soft flesh of her buttocks, holding her hips against his own.

"Case," she murmured, telling him in the sound of his name that he had to fulfill the promise of passion his body had made her.

Slowly and reluctantly he lowered her until her feet rested on solid ground again. Without speaking further, they left the crowded enclosure and walked back along the rickety wooden docks to the portion of the marina where the schooner and the ketch were tied up.

With Megan's hand clasped tightly in his, Case dealt with his jumble of emotions. As the blare of the music receded into the background he told himself first that he hadn't meant this to happen tonight. It had already become more than apparent that sex did nothing to settle the issues separating Megan and himself.

Liar, he accused himself. *You meant this to happen. You want her. You'll always want her, no matter what your judgment tells you.*

The honesty of the admission loosened something tight and snarled inside Case. The relief made it possible for him to put the future aside. Tonight he and Megan were together. He would savor that, luxuriate in it, penetrate its depths. Tomorrow he would deal with tomorrow.

Megan was grateful that Case didn't say anything to deny their mutual urgency when they stepped aboard the moored yacht that had been their floating hotel the past week and a half. There was a wonderful honesty in the way they walked silently through the main salon to Case's stateroom. He opened the door and waited for her to enter.

She walked several steps past him and turned, her face and eyes luminous with the sense of "rightness." This time was different from the other times they had made love on this trip. Tonight there was no subterfuge, no seduction, open or subtle. They simply needed each other and were here to give of themselves and receive in turn.

"Case—" she began softly, succumbing to the urge to express something of what trembled inside her.

"No," he said swiftly, coming over to her and taking her into his arms. She understood at once and complied. He was asking that they have no words tonight, no questions, no explanations or apologies, no promises. Just the unspoken messages their bodies would exchange, messages of passion and love.

Megan slipped her arms up around his neck and lifted her face in readiness for his kiss, expecting it to be deep and possessive and familiar. Instead he lowered his head very slowly, as though making the overture for the first time. His lips explored the soft shape of hers the way one would nuzzle the individual petals of a rose to discover their satin fragrance and graceful symmetry. The sensation that bloomed inside Megan was strange and delightful.

She held herself absolutely still while Case explored her entire face with the same gentle curiosity. He dropped little feather kisses at the corners of her

mouth, in the faint hollows underneath her cheek-
bones and then on each closed lid. Megan found that
she was holding her breath, not with a sense of
urgency or an eagerness for deepening intensity but
with the sheer pleasure of his leisure.

Her hands dropped away from his neck as he
raised his head and continued the exploration of the
rest of her with his hands. He stroked the softness of
her hair and the curve of her neck and shoulders,
sliding the narrow straps of her sundress down over
the tops of her arms almost as a matter of course.
When his fingers dropped to the buttons at the front
of her dress, Megan stood like a docile child about to
be undressed, her pulse fluttering with excitement as
he undid the buttons one by one and then dropped
the dress around her feet.

His dark gaze felt like an admiring caress as it
moved over her small, curvaceous figure, attired
only in brief bikini panties, and returned to focus on
her rounded breasts, the ruddy aureole on each tip
surrounding a timid nipple. With the fingertips of
both hands, he lightly traced the undercurve of each
breast and then followed the outline of her body as
though he were tracing her on cardboard, sliding his
palms from beneath her arms down to the tapering
slimness of her waist and then outward over her
hips. A small shudder of a sigh escaped Megan's lips
as he knelt in front of her and continued the
downward exploration, sliding his hands along the
outsides of her rounded thighs and then further
down over her calves and ankles.

Wherever he touched her, he set off silvery rockets of sensation until Megan had the illusion that she was bit by bit turning incandescent. At her ankles he curved his hands around to the backs and worked his way lightly upward, spending seconds savoring the shape of her shapely buttocks under their thin nylon covering. He gradually rose as he smoothed his palms upward over the planes of her back to her shoulders, having completed the initial surface tour.

"Case," she murmured as he bent and kissed the peak of one breast, the feather touch bringing the nipple out of hiding in a brazen fashion. With his hands placed flat on her back and idle in a way she deeply regretted, he tasted her breasts thoroughly with his lips and tongue and then very gently with his teeth. Megan arched into him, that part of her he hadn't touched aching now and demanding its share of attention. Unable to contain herself any longer, she grasped his shoulders with both hands to communicate her urgency, feeling as she did so the cloth of his shirt over the ridged muscles.

"Case, you're driving me crazy!" she muttered, pulling at the shirt.

But he wasn't to be hurried. He was like a man on a virgin hike through an untraveled forest. He wanted to discover every marvel in singular detail. After he had feasted at her breasts, he put his hands in motion again, sliding them down and easing her panties past her hips and letting them drop to her ankles. Megan trembled in anticipation as he kissed the curving line of her waist and hips, driving her to distraction when his tongue made a foray into her navel. She groaned aloud when he arrived at length to that juncture where her legs met and where all the pent-up sexual longing was concentrated. But as he parted her thighs with his stroking hands, he seemed content to kiss the tender flesh along the insides of her thighs, coming so close to that throbbing, aching center that finally her control snapped. She grabbed his head and forced the intimacy that kept eluding her. But such weakness invaded her trembling legs at the first flick of his warm, rough tongue into the heated crevice of her desire that Megan found she didn't have the strength to stand.

"Case, please . . ." she begged in a murmur, sinking down to the cabin floor.

His hands were slipping under her buttocks, lifting her for his slow, maddening consumption. Megan opened herself fully to him, writhing and crying out with the pleasure shooting through her with each stroke of his tongue. He was hitting directly upon the white-hot center of the volcanic mass of desire that had once been her pelvis. She felt the first rumblings of release and cried out his name as one convulsion engendered another and then another, each more explosive than the last.

Megan was too limp and weak to render aid when Case tried to help her up from the floor. Comprehending her state, he slipped his arms under her and picked her up. After he had laid her on his bunk, she watched as he began to undress and then suddenly felt a resurgence of strength.

"No! Let me!" she ordered softly, getting up.

Her eyes held his with a sensual promise as she finished unbuttoning his shirt and slid it off. Next she removed his belt and undid the fastening of his trousers, taking her time as he had done with her. When she slid the trousers down over his hips, she knelt in front of him while he lifted each leg. Then she stayed there, noting the way the cotton material of his briefs stretched taut across the probing male shape. The sight rekindled her sexual excitement.

Looking up into his eyes, she lifted her hands to him slowly and caressed him lightly through the material, seeing the contortion of his features as he expelled a groan. Slipping her fingertips underneath the elastic waistband, she made a leisurely business of working the briefs gradually lower until finally she had freed that urgently male tumescence whose very shape symbolized aggressiveness. When he had stepped free of this one remaining garment and stood naked before her, she proceeded to lavish upon him the same kind of sensual torment she had suffered and enjoyed at his hands.

Her palms slid up the hairy roughness of his muscular legs, stopping to knead the thighs. He sucked in his breath as he watched her hands move very slowly to take possession of that most vulnerable part of his male anatomy. Feeling like Delilah with all of Samson's strength in the palm of her hand, Megan gently stroked and caressed him, furthering the devastation with her lips and tongue until she felt the shudders of passion in his body and he stopped her, grasping her by the shoulders and drawing her up to him.

"I want you," he said in a low, passion-husked voice. "I want to be inside you."

Megan wanted nothing more herself at that moment. She turned with him toward the bunk and lay on her back, holding her arms up to him as he bent over her.

The union was deep and explosive. There was no teasing now, no drawing out or prolonging of sensation. It was an elemental coming together of a man and a woman who had brought to each other already the full range of erotic pleasure. Now they plumbed each other for greater depths. With a driving force, Case surged into her, again and again, possessing her totally, carrying himself and her, too, to a plane of utter mindlessness where nothing existed but the two of them, forged by their white-hot passion into one.

During the weeks ahead, Megan would remember that night often, re-live it with a sense of wonder. Their lovemaking had had a newness and a sense of discovery. They might have been two lovers coming together for the first time with none of the usual awkwardness and uncertainty of how to please. There had also been the depth and completeness that comes only with time and familiarity and caring. That final coming together had been an immutable statement of the sharing of certain essentials of life they would always find in each other, regardless of those differences that had wedged them apart the past two years.

On the flight home Megan found herself thinking that while nothing had been settled between herself and Case on this trip, her own understanding of herself and him had been deepened. She was returning home a different person in some respects. Not that she had miraculously discovered the desire to turn back the clock and resume the role of happy housewife once again. That was not the situation at all. But she knew she was going to put every ounce of energy and intelligence into saving her marriage to Case. No longer was she going to hold herself proudly aloof and wait for him to come around.

For the first time, she realized Case hadn't been without his inner dissatisfactions during those years she had cleaned his house, cooked his meals, and waited home for him. She had always wrongly assumed that he was completely fulfilled in his career, a fantastically successful career that had brought him recognition and lucrative pay. Apparently the whole time he had felt he was sacrificing himself for the good of his family. Megan wondered if that sense of martyrdom wasn't connected in some way with his adamant insistence that she keep within the narrow confines of the role he had assigned her, the dependent wife whose needs are all supplied by her hard-working husband.

She intended to talk about all these things when Case came back to New York. Once she had given only half-serious consideration to the idea of professional counseling. Now she thought it might be necessary.

In the meanwhile she had to go home and plunge herself into the task of writing the feature. Her mother and the two children would want to know all about her trip. She was eager to reassure herself about the condition of Danny's leg and ease whatever mental anxieties the injury had caused him. All this plus the constant thought of Case. . . . She wouldn't have to worry about time hanging heavy on her hands.

Chapter Eleven

*M*egan picked up her office extension and briefly identified herself, wondering as she did so how many calls she'd had that day. It seemed like at least a thousand, but she would have been an ingrate to complain when many of them had been calls from friends and former colleagues with glowing accolades for Megan's terrific work on the Caribbean feature, which had just appeared in this month's issue of *Today's Fashion*.

"Of *course* I remember you, Val! Don't be silly!" she admonished this latest caller. Mentally she visualized the tall, willowy young blonde as she listened to her extravagant praise of Megan's feature article, which she had entitled "Caribbean Idyll, or Eden

Revisited." Megan had admired Val's aggressive technique for mingling with her editorial superiors the night of that fateful party when Megan and Case saw each other again for the first time in two years, the night when doors began to open for Megan.

"I'd love to get together for lunch soon, Val," Megan assured her former colleague at the close of the conversation. After thanking her for calling and hanging up, Megan slumped forward with a groan of fatigue, resting her forehead on the heels of her palms. God, what a day! In just thirty minutes she had an editorial staff meeting and needed to be clearing her desk instead of just sitting there, but the call from Val brought to mind just how much *had* happened in the last five months.

Looking back, Megan felt as though she had been poised on the threshold of her future that night of the party, without really knowing it at the time. Now she had both feet solidly planted on a lower rung of that notoriously slippery editorial ladder in the world of women's magazine publishing. Her position as assistant editor of the travel section in *Today's Fashion* was secure with the future promising more opportunities for advancement. Dee Gardner had been overwhelmingly enthusiastic about Megan's work on the Caribbean feature.

"When I see Case Ballantine again, I plan to tell him he did me a big favor after all, the big bully," Dee had told Megan earlier the same day. The editor-in-chief's meaningful smile had only deepened the mystification of several other curious staff members within easy hearing distance.

The words had fallen like sharp-edged stones on a

sensitive spot inside Megan, a spot that grew increasingly raw with the passage of each day and week. It was all she could do not to make some bitterly sarcastic remark Dee wouldn't understand such as "If you *do* see Case, be sure to give him *my* best." But aside from not wanting to give Dee food for speculation, Megan was too filled with anxiety to be allowed the relief of venting her impatience and frustration with verbal outbursts. Deep down she was worried sick about Case.

Six weeks had passed since she had left him in Grenada. Aside from the infrequent postcard addressed to both her and the children, he hadn't communicated with her. What was he *doing* all this time, she wondered with both exasperation and uneasiness. Surely Alina must have returned from France by now, or even if she had not, Jacques would meet with no serious difficulty in signing on temporary crew members more experienced than Case. The islands had been full of adventuresome young sailors willing to sign on as crew of a fine cruising yacht such as *l'Esprit* with little more compensation than a berth and meals.

The islands had had more than a few adventuresome sailors not so young, Megan was forced to remind herself before she summarily brushed aside the absurd notion that Case might not be coming back at all. A man like Case wasn't capable of "dropping out" of the mainstream of society, she told herself. He was too solid and responsible a person ever to abandon his parental obligations, but aside from that, he possessed too much creative energy to be content with drifting from year to year in an existence that had only survival and random experience as its purpose for being. Case was definitely coming back. It was a matter of *when*.

After she had emphatically reassured herself of his eventual return, Megan was left with a vague shadow of worry and an aching frustration that erupted periodically into spurts of anger. It was patently unfair of Case to leave her at loose ends while he sailed around the Caribbean all winter sorting out his thoughts! What about *her* and her thoughts!

She had flown back to the States filled with such high hopes that as soon as he had had his respite from the pressures of his work, he would return home and they would work out their problems so that they could get on with the business of the future. But now her patience had begun to grow thinner and thinner by the day. She needed to see him, to touch him, to know that he was all right mentally and physically, to sit down with him and pour out all the hopes and fears and longings inside her. Caught up as she was in the frustrating sense of waiting, she couldn't even take full pleasure in her professional triumph. If only Case were here, her satisfaction in having done a good job on the feature and having been recognized for it would be far more complete.

"Damn you, Case Ballantine! Why don't you come home!" Megan muttered under her breath, rousing herself with an effort from the inertia of introspection. Glancing at her watch to verify that only twenty minutes now remained before she was due to attend the staff meeting, she began to straighten the clutter on her desk.

So absorbed was she in her task that she was

unaware of the visitor who appeared in the doorway and hesitated. He might have been summoning his courage as he studied her with an intent gaze and then gave the cubicle of an office a sweeping survey before making a throat-clearing sound to alert her of his presence.

Megan glanced around, caught her breath in surprise, and blinked as though to make sure he wasn't a mirage.

"Case!" she blurted out, staring hard at him and making the adjustment to his unexpected appearance. It was as though thinking about him with such intensity as she had just been doing had produced him in the flesh.

"Sorry to barge in and startle you like this," Case apologized casually, coming over and dropping into a chair near her desk before she could gather her wits enough to get up and go to him.

"It's all right! Don't be silly!" she hastened to assure him, her eyes going over him hungrily and noting the deeply bronzed hue of his face and hands. The rest of him underneath the dark slacks and bulky turtleneck sweater would be just as suntanned.

"God, you look fantastic. When did you get back? Why didn't you call me? Where have you *been* all this time?" As the words tumbled out of her, Megan was uncomfortably aware that she looked a mess. Her hair was probably standing on end, the way she'd been combing her fingers through it, as she unconsciously did when she was exasperated. And her makeup definitely could use some retouching.

Case didn't seem to hear the urgent stream of

questions. He reached over and picked up the copy of *Today's Fashion* lying on her desk and flipped carefully through it until he had come to the travel section and her feature with his photographs.

"Great job, Meg," he complimented with quiet sincerity. "Dee Gardner had to have been pleased with it."

"Oh, she was!" Megan replied quickly, stifling a wave of uneasiness she didn't understand since it had no basis. She had every reason to be ecstatic. Case was sitting right here in her office, looking fit and vital, his beard and hair neatly trimmed. So what if he hadn't swept into her office and taken her into his arms. This was life, not a soap opera. The two of them had been through some rough times the last two and a half years. There was talking yet to be done, barriers to be removed, concessions to be made. *Why did Case seem to be looking anywhere but directly at her?*

"Needless to say Dee was thrilled with your pictures, too," Megan pointed out, not at all sure why she wanted to switch the focus away from herself and her work on the feature. "When did you see the final product of our labors, anyway? In the airport?"

It was the perfect opening for Case to get back to all those questions he hadn't answered yet about when he had arrived in New York and why he had been so long in getting there. But he seemed so intent on the magazine article he might have been seeing it for the first time.

"I had a copy of the magazine in my mail. Dee

must have sent it to me." Case turned back to the
first page of the article. "'Caribbean Idyll or Eden
Revisited'," he read aloud in a meditative tone. "By
Megan O'Riley."

"Photographs by Case Ballantine," Megan added,
her heartbeat suddenly accelerating with a strange
sense of foreboding. Why wouldn't Case *look* at
her? Whatever was wrong obviously had something
to do with the feature and she could guess what it
was. "You don't know how tempted I was to let the
cat out of the bag and use my real name, Megan
O'Riley Ballantine," she said regretfully. "But the
situation was so awkward. I didn't quite have the
nerve, especially since you weren't here for me to
ask if you minded." The loud sigh was designed to
get his attention. "I took the coward's way out and
just let things ride for the time being."

Case glanced up at her briefly, looked around the
small office and then back down at the glossy pages
of the magazine in his hands. Before he could speak,
Megan was plunging on in a panicky attempt to
eliminate the alarming sense of wrongness about this
first meeting she had so been looking forward to for
weeks.

"The only reason I used my maiden name in the
first place, Case, was that I was determined not to
take advantage of *your* name and reputation. I
wanted to get that first job completely on my own
and prove my own ability. Thanks to you and the
opportunity you got for me with Dee Gardner, I've
been able to show what I *can* do. But it's never felt
right, having people think of me as Megan O'Riley.

Deep down I've been Megan Ballantine all along."
I've been your wife even when we weren't living together.

Case only half listened to the words. He was disturbingly aware of all she wasn't saying as well as what she was. The faint undertone of uncertainty told him she sensed something was wrong and wanted to dispel whatever it was. A bleak sadness welled up inside him as he realized Megan was hoping for the impossible. She wanted him to say they could just forget the problems of the past two and a half years and proceed to live happily ever after, everything miraculously right between them, all the hurt eased away, all the scars healed. If only he could honestly tell her all that instead of what he had come to tell her today. The kindest thing he could do for both of them was to dispense with the preliminaries and get this over with.

"It's probably better that you used your maiden name and people don't know we're married," he said, raising his head as he spoke and finally meeting her gaze steadily, his eyes dark with somber purpose. "I want a divorce, Meg."

Megan stared back at him, the strength and vitality rushing out of her body with her expelled breath until she was empty, a thin, brittle shell.

"You want a divorce," she echoed in an unbelieving voice that was just barely audible.

Case quickly dropped his gaze to that damned magazine he was gripping now in fingers as tense as steel. Deliberately he forced himself to read the title and the byline of the feature, both of them distortions of the truth, reminders of a world of superficiality he had spurned totally in his mind now and was determined to leave behind him. Since that world meant so much to Megan, even more than he did, he would have to leave her behind, too. Divorce was the only answer.

"Don't worry," Case said sternly, sitting up straight in the chair and tossing the magazine back on her desk. It landed with a decisive little *plop*. "I've been working with my attorney the last week setting things up for you and the kids." He steeled himself as the shock in Megan's eyes darkened with hurt and accusation at this revelation. "It actually came as a surprise that I was worth so much money," he went on quickly, making an effort at the lightness of irony. "But then I guess we never really got around to developing extravagant tastes, did we?"

The expression on Megan's face was more than Case could bear. She looked like a victim of shock, paralyzed into a sitting position. Except for her eyes, which were trained on him with a terrible intensity, widened with horror and disbelief, she showed no evidence of feeling or life. Getting up abruptly from his chair, Case walked over to the wall and fixed his gaze unseeingly on a print while he continued to outline the plans he had made for taking care of her and the two children.

"There'll be trust funds for Kathleen and Danny, to cover their college education. The rest will be invested in your name. With the income from that plus your salary, which should be going up all the time, I don't see any reason you and the kids should have to lower your standard of living."

Case took a chance and turned around, only to

discover that Megan hadn't moved a fraction of an inch, nor had her expression changed. He was genuinely worried about her. She had never reacted like this to any kind of crisis or distressing news. Megan was the kind to weep and get hysterical or angry, the kind to vent her feelings, not to act like a zombie. Case wasn't even really sure she was hearing him.

"Now that the kids are getting older and their interests are changing, you might want to consider selling the house and buying something a little easier on upkeep—" Case broke off and swung away from her again as her face crumpled with pain. "Of course, it's not up to me to tell you what to do," he added tersely, waiting for the storm finally to break.

"Sell the house . . . but you *love* that house . . ." Megan murmured to his back in a broken, stricken little voice. This was all a terrible nightmare. She was going to wake up any second now and find out she had been dreaming. "I've been waiting for you all these weeks, Case, thinking about our future together—how we were going to work things out—be together again—and the whole time *you—*" Megan's voice cracked, an inadequate vehicle for the intensity of her emotion. She reached deep within herself for resources of strength she had never tapped before, not even that awful day when she had feared the worst about Danny. Case had been beside her, lending her his strength. Now she was terribly alone.

"Case. *Please*. Would you sit down and *look* at me," she pleaded in a voice ragged with desperation.

It seemed to take an eternity for him to turn slowly around and sit once again in the chair. His face was somber with regret and concern, but his eyes met hers unflinchingly, as she had requested. A new wave of despair hit her as she realized anew that he meant every word he had said. *He really wanted a divorce.*

"Why—" Megan began and then found herself unable to continue. She pressed a balled fist up against her trembling mouth to keep her whole face from crumpling again. That first numbness of shock was fast fading away now, taking with it her unnatural composure. She wanted to throw back her head and wail against this terrible thing Case was doing to them. She wanted to scream out protests that it simply couldn't be the way he was saying. The future was too horrible to encompass, a hideous giant canvas of blacks and grays and ugly clashing colors.

"I'm sorry, Meg. I truly am. I wish there could have been some easier way—for both of us." Case's voice was deep and heavy with compassion, but unwavering in his resolution. He had already been through the private Gethsemane of decision. "You see, I'm getting out of fashion photography altogether. I don't even know right now exactly what kind of photography I'll get into next or where it will be. I do know for sure it won't be New York and it won't have anything to do with models strutting around in ridiculous costumes. I've had more than enough of that to last me the rest of my life."

Megan had felt herself grow calmer as Case talked, listening not just to the words but to the terrible tone of finality. The plans he mentioned had nothing to do with her. His hazy future was all *I*'s without a single *we*.

"But if you disliked fashion photography that much, why did you get into it in the first place?" Her question sounded mechanical, unconvincing, its only real purpose to break into that inexorable flow of words. "I never expected you to do anything you didn't want to do, Case. I certainly never asked you to sacrifice yourself in order to support me and the kids." Her voice was gradually gaining strength, becoming reproachful. "Is it fair now to blame *me*, to blame *them?*"

The return of her spirit came as an immense relief to Case. "I'm not blaming anybody, Meg," he denied firmly. "Please don't ever think that. I did what I did out of choice, and I'm not sorry. But it's all past history now. Maybe I'm just kidding myself, but I want the clean slate, the fresh page. Please don't get me wrong," he added quickly when she drew her breath in sharply and was about to interrupt him. "I'll always be Kathleen and Danny's father. I'll keep in touch with them, wherever I go. I'll spend as much time with them as I can. I want to be a part of their lives. But right now you have more to offer them on a stable basis than I do. It's the sensible thing that they stay with you."

Megan opened her mouth again to interrupt him, but Case only spoke faster, as though in a hurry to get everything said that he had come to say. "You'll see, too, when we both sit down with our attorneys and settle the property that the kids will be well provided for—so will you, for that matter. I'm not keeping much for myself, just enough to keep me going for six months or so. I'll always be able to make enough money for just me. But I won't be able to pay much child support, not for a while anyway."

He had finally stopped, leaving a space open for her to speak. Megan felt overwhelmed by the sheer volume of all the words. She didn't quite know where to start in opposing the elaborate structure of his plans. Wiping one hand across her face in a weary gesture, as though to clear away her expression with all its conflicting emotion, she started as her telephone console emitted its space-age sound that had replaced the simple bell and the buzzer.

"Excuse me," she said quietly, picking up the receiver. "Yes," she answered briefly and listened, a look of dismay spreading over her features. "The meeting. No, I haven't forgotten it, Kate," she lied. "But I'll be late. Something urgent's come up that I have to see to."

Case heard her words with the deepest kind of relief. At the risk of admitting his cowardice, he wanted to get out of here at once. He didn't know how much more either he or Megan could take. With a flash of insight, he realized he had chosen to come here to her office today to break the news that he wanted a divorce, knowing there would probably be interruptions when they were most needed. It had also seemed appropriate to him for this meeting to take place in the environment she gave first importance in her life. To experience firsthand the demands her career made upon her attention and time and energy helped to reinforce his decision. He and Megan would probably always love each other, but they were on two different wavelengths, people with different values headed in different directions.

"I won't keep you from your meeting." Case grasped the arms of the chair in preparation for rising.

"No—don't go—" Megan jerked forward, her body poised to spring at him if he failed to heed her voice. "I don't care about the meeting," she added urgently. "It's not important." An emphatic motion with one hand dismissed the staff meeting and shoved it over into a corner of the little office.

Noting with relief that Case's fingers, deep mahogany and suggesting human warmth against the gleam of stainless steel, had relaxed their grip on the arms of the chair, Megan settled back slowly. For some incomprehensible reason his obvious reluctance in delaying his departure was heartening. She was struck suddenly with an entirely new perception that brought with it hope. By his own admission Case had been in New York a week without contacting her. During that time he had consulted with an attorney and set about making financial provisions for her and the children even before he told her he wanted a divorce. Why? Case was not a man who lacked the courage to defend his convictions. The past two and a half years were ample proof of that. *Was he really as sure of himself in making this permanent break as he seemed to be?* Had he been taking all these steps toward divorce to bolster his decision?

"Case, when did you decide all this?" Megan asked in a gravely matter-of-fact voice, totally composed now as she awaited his answer. When he frowned and lifted one hand in an impatient gesture, about to ask what difference it made, she went on reflectively. "You told me at that party last September, when we ran into each other, that you wanted us to get back together again, to be a family. And then you got me the writing assignment with Dee and we went down to the islands." Megan's voice softened. "We had some beautiful times there together. I think I would have *known* . . ." She summoned all her nerve. "Case, was it something that happened after I left you in Grenada? Did you meet somebody?"

To her immense relief his denial was clear on his face even before he shook his head impatiently and gave her the answer she longed to hear.

"No, I didn't meet anybody. There's no 'other woman,' Meg." Case shifted restlessly. "It's hard to say exactly *when* I knew things weren't ever going to work out for us. You don't just decide something like that overnight or in a flash of insight. I was pretty damned miserable the last couple of years, as you know. The whole time I kept thinking we could go back to the way things were *before* . . . before you got the job here in the city . . . hell, before that, too, I guess, looking back. It just finally dawned on me while we were down in the islands that things never were going to be the way I hoped they would be. We were never going to 'go back.' I don't think people ever do."

Chills rippled down Megan's backbone at the bleakness in his face and in his voice as he made these grave pronouncements. It took all her strength to resist his awful certainty. God help her, she *couldn't* believe him! She *couldn't* give up! It was of the most vital importance that she probe and question and bring everything out into the open, no matter how painful the process to both of them.

"It was my decision to stay and finish the feature that decided you, wasn't it?" She watched him as he looked inward, remembering. "You were terribly disappointed that I didn't go home to Danny, weren't you? And yet when I gave you the opportunity to influence me, you wouldn't. Quite the contrary, in fact. You pointed out that Danny wasn't seriously ill and could get along without me for several more days."

Case nodded slowly.

"I guess you're right. When you decided to stay, I remember feeling like something went dead inside me. Not that I think even at this moment that you were wrong or a bad mother. I just finally got it through my thick head that your career was that *important* to you. It wasn't something you would lose interest in and give up after a while." Case gestured toward the magazine lying on top of the desk. "And you're good. That article's proof of it. You'll go places and be as successful as you want to be." He paused, his face falling into lines of wisdom and sadness that made him look older than his thirty-eight years. "Success comes at a high price, Meg. I just want you to know that. It demands the best of what you've got in you, and the job has to come first. I think you got a taste of what the cost is when you had to decide whether to come home to Danny or stay and finish the job."

"I *did!*" Megan burst out. "It was horrible! Case, I didn't try to hide that from you at the time! Afterward I wanted so much to talk about it, but you shut me out. I wanted to ask you if it isn't the same way for men. Don't *they* have to put the job first, too? Didn't *you?* You said yourself there were lots of times you wished you could come home when you called and found out I was in the middle of some crisis."

Case shoved his hands farther along the arms of his chair, seeking the coolness of the hard metal not yet warmed by his flesh. The vehemence of her voice had come as a relief, reassuring him that Megan was tough and resilient. She would be all right. This was all coming as a shock to her, but in a short time she would get over it and devote herself to the career that was so important to her.

"Of course it's the same for men," he agreed a little wearily. "Sure there were times—more than I care to remember—when it tore at my guts not to be able to take the first plane home. And all you would have had to do was ask me, and nothing could have stopped me. But you always insisted that you could handle whatever it was. And I had confidence that you would." Case hesitated, finding himself having to verbalize what he'd never really put into words before because it had simply been understood as far as he was concerned.

"I always felt that you and I were partners with different roles in the same business. Whatever I had to *do* . . . whatever I had to give up—like taking the pictures I would rather be taking or being at home with you and the kids—well, that was just my part of the deal. I was doing what I could do, the best I could do it, for *us*—for you and me and the kids." He shifted in his chair again and shrugged, finding the going entirely too awkward. "Now that's all changed."

Megan was staring at him, feeling strangely as though she were gazing at a totally familiar scene through a clarifying lens. Everything was the same and yet different. All those years what Case was telling her now had been so plain, but she hadn't been able to see it.

"In your mind, I stopped holding up my end of the deal," she said slowly. "You didn't mind working at a profession you really wouldn't have chosen for yourself as long as *I* was willing to make the same kind of concessions and sacrifices. No, it's true, Case," she added hurriedly when he would have interrupted and denied what she was saying. "I've never really seen it before. I've never really understood why you objected so strongly to my having my own career."

And now that she did see and did understand, Megan was at a loss at how to deal with the situation because there were so many complex questions to answer. Did Case's love for her hinge on her being that "partner" he had married in the first place? Could their relationship change and adjust to individual growth? Before Megan could delve further into the emotional tangle, the telephone sounded peremptorily.

"Damn!" Megan muttered, aware of Case's close scrutiny as she lifted the receiver. Before she even had a chance to speak one word into it, Dee Gardner's raspy smoker's voice was in the room, clear to her and Case.

"Megan, what the hell's holding you up? We're all here waiting for you."

"I'm sorry, Dee. I'll be there as soon as I can—" Megan broke off, hearing the click and the quiet drone that said Dee had hung up without waiting for an answer. "Case, *please! Don't go!*" she begged helplessly as he got up, a look of determination on his face saying that he wouldn't be swayed into staying longer this time.

"There's really not much more to say, Meg, is there?" He glanced pointedly at the telephone and then quickly around the office. "You have your meeting and I have a hundred and one things to do. All the talk in the world can't change the facts. I want a divorce. As soon as the attorney has all the details worked out, I'll be in touch with you. We'll need to get together with him and your attorney and make everything legal."

It seemed to Megan that Case intended just to stride out of her office without a further word, but he halted at the door and spoke over his shoulder, not looking at her.

"So long . . . and take care."

Megan sat staring at the empty doorway, biting

her lip and wrestling with the violent clash of impulses that kept her from doing anything at all. Part of her urged to forget the damned meeting and run after him. But she didn't know at this point what she could say to change his mind. He seemed so adamant about getting a divorce. And with each passing moment her resentment grew as she realized just how blatantly unfair Case had been, coming to her office during working hours to tell her news of the most devastating importance when he knew there would almost certainly be interruptions. And then to leave the clear implication as he had done just before leaving that her job's rightful claims upon her time were indisputable proof that the job meant more to her than *he* did.

Right up to the bitter end, Case was determined to prove his point—Megan couldn't manage a career and marriage to him at the same time. How could one reason with a man like that?

Overwhelmed with frustration and the seeming hopelessness of her situation, Megan reached over and picked up the magazine on her desk and hurled it viciously to the floor. The display cracked the awful tension inside her. Tears began to slide down her face.

"Damn you, Case Ballantine!" she murmured brokenly, standing and slowly gathering up a stack of folders in her arms. *Damn* Dee Gardner and her *damned* meeting, too! *Damn* every cockeyed thing in this cockeyed world!

Megan's vehement denunciations did nothing to change things. Dee and the other editors were waiting for her. Her personal world might be in a million fragments, but it wasn't their fault. She had her job to do, her career to consider. And right now it was much easier just to do what was demanded of her. She was momentarily incapable of self-direction.

Chapter Twelve

*M*egan might as well not have gone to the meeting. She found it impossible to concentrate on the agenda. There she sat at a conference table where some of the top editorial talent in the entire country made decisions shaping the future issues of *Today's Fashion,* and Megan simply couldn't find it in herself to care.

She felt so empty, so terribly empty.

Just a few short months ago, she had yearned to be sitting precisely in the chair she now occupied, sure that nothing else in the world could give her more satisfaction at this stage in her career. Now she found herself thinking that without Case, what meaning would her job have for her? What meaning would *anything* have?

Why had she never asked herself this question before?

The answer was instantly forthcoming. Never once during the two and a half years she had lived apart from Case had she ever really believed that either of them would terminate the ties that bound them together, ties she had considered permanent. In her mind, Case had always been accessible to her even when they both took such care to avoid seeing each other. He was a stable, dependable part of her life, but even more than that, the person she knew would care about her and be concerned about her welfare in spite of bitter differences.

You fool! Megan derided herself scornfully. *You stupid blind fool!* As the chilling prospect of divorce seeped through her brain she realized she had been careless with what now seemed more precious than anything else in life, her marriage to Case. And now it might be too late for her to save it. *But I can't live without Case.*

"Megan, you're a million miles away." Dee Gardner's strident voice broke into Megan's tortured self-searching. "You look like you've just lost your best friend," the editor-in-chief added chidingly.

Megan mustered a wan smile but her usually vivid blue eyes were dull with misery. "I have, Dee," she said sadly. "I have."

As a stir rippled through the assembly of editors, Megan pushed back her chair and stood up. "I'm sorry," she said with quiet dignity, "but you'll have to excuse me." With no more explanation, she walked out of the room.

Halfway to her office, Megan remembered the stack of folders she had left behind, but didn't go back to retrieve them. They really didn't matter to her just now. The one thing that did matter was getting in touch with Case at once and telling him divorce was out of the question. She wouldn't agree to it. Their relationship had proved not to be as tough nor as durable as she had wrongly assumed it was, but still it was too vital to her happiness—to his, too, she hoped—just to relinquish it to the refuse heap of divorce. She would do anything—*anything* at all, she meant to tell him—to save their marriage.

With nothing more specific to offer in the way of solutions to their problems than this unqualified offer, which Megan probably secretly hoped was enough in itself, she closed herself into her little office and set about trying to locate Case. Her fingers trembled with her urgency as she picked up the telephone and dialed his apartment first. No answer. Next she dialed the number of his studio, knowing that he never answered the phone there himself but expecting to get his answering service. Instead there was a recording informing her that the number had been disconnected.

Megan hung up the phone and sat motionless, an irrational panic sweeping through her at this surprising evidence of Case's haste in burning his bridges. She *had* to get in touch with him, but how? She couldn't tell him anything until she managed to locate him, and in the meantime, God knows what other drastic steps he would take.

"The attorney!" she muttered as the thought struck that Case might have left her and gone straight to the office of his legal counsel. Or even if he hadn't, considering the rush he seemed to be in to change his life, he would certainly be in touch with the attorney.

Jerking open a drawer, Megan got out her handbag and searched in it for the little book of addresses and telephone numbers, knowing even as she did so that Case might have gone to someone other than their family attorney. When husband and wife were getting a divorce, they frequently used attorneys with whom neither had had previous dealings to avoid conflicts of interest. In this instance, however, there would be no reason for that. Case had indicated he was being more than generous and giving her and the children nearly everything.

"Bentley. Arnold Bentley," Megan muttered aloud, flipping nervously through the pages of the little book and locating the name and number she sought.

"I'm sorry. Mr. Bentley has left the office for the day," a cool professional female voice informed her. And no, Mr. Bentley's secretary insisted firmly, there was no number at which Mr. Bentley could be reached, but Mrs. Ballantine was welcome to leave a message.

It took all Megan's self-control to restrain her frustration at this newest obstacle. She wanted to shout at the woman, who was really only doing her job, not purposefully thwarting Megan.

"Tell Mr. Bentley I need to get in touch with my

husband right away. It's *urgent. Please* make that clear to him!"

The texture of the silence at the other end told Megan that the secretary was slightly disapproving of this display of emotion. Megan's voice had been frankly pleading with an undertone of desperation. In her present emotional state she was past caring about the sensibilities or the conjectures of strangers. After giving the secretary her number at the office and the one at home, Megan stressed that the attorney was to call her at the earliest opportunity, no matter what the hour.

After she had hung up, Megan lectured herself for giving into the feeling of panic that made her want to scream at people who weren't responsible for her problems. She had to stifle the urge to call anyone she could think of who knew Case, just on the chance that someone might have an inkling of his whereabouts.

Just be calm, she told herself. *Be patient.* Case could be any number of places. The fact that he hadn't answered the telephone at his apartment *didn't* mean he had moved out of it. The phone *had* rung. There hadn't been a recorded message.

Faced with the immediate decision of what to do next, Megan found that she couldn't bring herself to leave the city without at least trying to find him. Knowing all the while that the search was futile, she went first to his apartment and then to his studio. Finding him at neither place, she went home where she waited for a call from the attorney and rang Case's home phone at regular intervals.

Now there was time to think. Time to go over and

over the scene with Case in her office. Megan tried to recall every word, every nuance, every expression on Case's face. Emotionally she experienced again the shock, the disbelief, the feeling that her life was being yanked up by the roots. She also felt again the welling indignation that Case had chosen that particular time and place to tell her. Once she'd relived the whole nightmare, she was left with the same sense of urgency. She *had* to talk to Case. With every minute and hour that ticked by, their relationship might be in even greater peril as Case took one step after another to sever the bonds connecting them.

It might already be too late . . .

As time crawled by, Megan did battle with that insidious possibility. That evening, out of sheer necessity, she mastered a kind of self-discipline that had never been her strong suit: patience. Time and time again she dialed the number of Case's apartment and listened to the ring that could go on into infinity. When her own phone would ring, she would run to answer it, thinking that Arnold Bentley might be calling.

And like any mother with children in the house, she was denied the luxury of dwelling exclusively upon her own thoughts and concerns, which in this instance were her children's concerns, too, even if they were unaware of the peril. Kathleen was absorbed in devising a totally new and glamorous hairdo for herself. She kept appearing to demand Megan's opinion.

"What do you think, Mom?" she wanted to know on the third trip from her bedroom into the large, cozy family room at the back of the house where Megan sat after supper, a magazine in her lap and the television playing, unheeded.

Megan obligingly studied the latest effort. Kathleen had swept her thick, lustrous shoulder-length hair back from her face and fastened it at each crown with barettes. It was apparent that she had also, without asking, experimented with some of Megan's makeup. Her eyelids were pale blue and her lashes startlingly long with mascara.

Megan didn't scold. She was too taken aback at this sudden glimpse of an older Kathleen, who from this preview would be a stunning young woman in a few short years. Megan was stirred by the bittersweet poignance a mother feels when she perceives the reality of her children's growing up. She wished with all her heart that Case were there this moment, sitting beside her on the sofa.

"It's becoming, honey," she complimented honestly. "Be sure to wash off that makeup before you go to bed."

Kathleen had the grace to blush. "I will," she agreed jauntily and then slid her mother a measuring glance. "Did I tell you Mary Lou Mason's mother lets her wear lipstick to school?" she queried in the tone of one who bears the burden of a much less reasonable mother than Mary Lou Mason's.

"I believe you have mentioned that fact," Megan said drily. "Now I think it's time for you to get ready for bed. Check on your brother for me, will you, and see if he's still procrastinating over that math homework."

With a little pout of the soft young lips that

needed no artificial color to make them lovely, Kathleen pivoted and sashayed from the room.

"Mom wants you," Megan heard her say out in the hall. The faintly patronizing tone was the one she reserved for her younger brother, who apparently was already on his way to the family room.

Megan smiled tenderly at her diminutive son as he appeared in the doorway. He had always seemed so much more vulnerable than Kathleen. In denim jeans and a gray sweatshirt with "CELTICS" written across the front, he trudged in sockfeet across the room toward Megan, his fine rust-colored hair tousled and his brown eyes thoughtful in their usual expression.

"Finished your homework, honey?" Megan tried to make her voice sound cheerfully matter-of-fact. It was a constant struggle for her not to be the overprotective mother with Danny. Case had warned her more than once not to make a mamma's boy out of him. "Is your leg bothering you?" she couldn't keep from asking as she noticed the careful way he placed one foot in front of the other.

"Uh, uh," he denied, shaking his head. "It just feels funny without the cast. Like it's too light or something."

"Danny—" He stopped at the tone of her voice and eyed her inquiringly. "You're outgrowing those jeans, aren't you?" Megan demanded. "You must have grown two inches the last month."

Danny looked down and examined his exposed ankles with concentrated interest. He looked inordinately pleased with himself as he came the rest of the way and climbed up on the sofa next to his mother.

"Growing's *weird,* isn't it, Mom?" he mused. "You don't really feel it or know it's happening until all of a sudden."

"You're so right, honey," Megan concurred, struck with the wisdom of his words. *Out of the mouth of babes,* she reflected, remembering a night down in the islands. She and Case had sat in the cockpit of *l'Esprit,* miles apart in their thinking. Smarting at his failure to make love to her, oblivious to his doubts about his virility at that time, Megan had chattered on about Kathleen and Danny, aware of Case's deepening mood.

"The kids are growing up so damned fast," he had remarked heavily.

Megan understood now what he had been saying. He hadn't been lamenting the natural growing process or wishing to deny it to his children. He had simply been more aware than Megan of time as a precious commodity. She had been spending the weeks and months and years as freely as though they were limitless in their supply. *Case, I'm sorry. What time we've wasted.*

"Danny, it's time for bed," she told her son. "I'll come in and say good night in a few minutes."

He got up without argument and left the room. Seconds later the telephone rang, like a peal of hope. Megan jumped up and ran to answer it, her heart pounding with the wish that Case was calling her. Perhaps the attorney had managed to get in touch with him. Or perhaps he was responding to the urgent message her heart was sending out to him tonight.

"Mrs. Ballantine?" The voice was male, bland,

and professional. "Arnold Bentley here. You called my office today and left a message . . ." Implicit in the explanation was an apology for having called her at home at this hour.

"Yes, Mr. Bentley," Megan answered, overwhelmed with her disappointment. "This is Megan Ballantine. Thank you for calling. I've been trying to get in touch with my husband all afternoon and this evening. He doesn't answer the phone at his apartment. It's very urgent that I talk with him. I was hoping that you might know where he is."

"I see." The polite tone was infinitely cautious. "Is anything wrong?"

Megan's first instinct made her suspect the man knew where Case was and didn't intend to tell her. He had definitely sounded evasive. Then her common sense reminded her that as an attorney, he did not always deal with human beings at their most noble. If he handled divorce cases, he probably had good reason to be cautious with the spouses of clients. Divorce tended to bring out the worst in people.

"Everything is wrong, Mr. Bentley," she said bluntly. "I love my husband and I don't want a divorce. We need to see each other and talk things out before they go too far."

"I see," he said again, still polite but not nearly so cautious. "I'm afraid I can't be of much help to you in contacting your husband, Mrs. Ballantine. He left no address or telephone number where I could reach him. He simply gave me instructions as to what he wanted me to do and said that he would be returning from Oregon in two weeks. By then—"

"Oregon!" Megan ejaculated. "Did you say *Oregon?"*

The pause at the other end was more eloquent than words. Mr. Bentley feared he had been hasty in letting down his guard and assuming Mrs. Ballantine's state of mind to be rational and her intentions the best.

"Why, yes," he said finally, the caution back full force. "Mr. Ballantine didn't go into any detail about his plans, but he mentioned something about a photographic assignment. For a nature magazine, as I recall."

Megan managed somehow not to echo the key phrases of his revelation. It was too incredible to believe that Case had gone completely across the country without telling her he even intended to leave the city.

"Case said he would be back in two weeks." Megan spoke each word slowly and carefully. "He didn't give you an address or a number where he could be reached."

"That is correct," Mr. Bentley verified without hesitation, sounding relieved that such was the situation.

"Thank you, Mr. Bentley." Megan was thoughtful but brisk. "If my husband calls you from Oregon, please tell him that I urgently need to talk to him. Would you do that?"

"Should Mr. Ballantine call, I shall most certainly give him that message," Arnold Bentley promised.

Megan stayed awake all that night, never once even making the effort to sleep. There was too much to think about, too much to remember, too much to

decide. By the next morning she had thought everything through and knew what she had to do. It was a
big gamble. The stakes were impossibly high: everything or nothing. But it was a risk she had to take.

As soon as she arrived at her office she called
Arnold Bentley and was put through to him with
little delay.

"Mr. Bentley, I've changed my mind about some
of the things I told you last night," she lied crisply.
"There's no need to talk to my husband after all.
Just forget that message I asked you to give him if he
called. I'll be waiting for definite word from you
about the date for the property settlement. Thank
you, Mr. Bentley. Have a nice day."

Chapter Thirteen

*M*egan dressed with painstaking care on this crucial day in her life. Following her instincts, she wore not one of her smart business suits but a simple, feminine dress of sheer navy wool that offset the lustrous choker of pearls Case had given her on their anniversary five years ago. The satin texture of the pearls against her throat infused some badly needed courage, but it didn't keep her fingers from trembling so hard that she had difficulty getting the matching pearl studs in her ears. Now that the day she had been awaiting with such urgency was finally here, she was scared silly.

What if the whole thing backfired in her face? What if Case heard her out and still wanted the divorce?

Those were questions Megan couldn't begin to answer, but they made her heart beat much too fast, her knees feel unsteady, and her eyes glitter with a feverish light.

Arnold Bentley's secretary showed Megan into a paneled conference room where Case and the attorney were already seated at one end of a long table that would easily have accommodated a dozen people. Both men arose as Megan entered.

As she walked from the door to the table and took the chair across from Case, Megan squeezed a polite greeting past a throat paralyzed with nervousness. Case looked so terribly grim and remote, as though prepared to get through an ordeal. He was uncharacteristically formal in a dark tweed suit, white shirt, and tie.

"Megan," he said somberly by way of greeting, increasing her terror when he used her full name rather than the shortened version he had called her ever since the day they met.

When they were all three seated, Arnold Bentley cleared his throat and opened the legal-sized folder in front of him. The sound did nothing to relieve the sharp tension in the room nor did it succeed in transferring to himself the attention of the other two people so that he could proceed in an orderly fashion with the business at hand.

"Bentley tells me you don't have an attorney to represent you." Case's statement was curt with disapproval, his tone threaded with accusation that wouldn't have made sense to an objective bystander. He was asking himself why in hell Megan had to show up here today looking so vulnerable and fragile and wearing the pearl necklace and earrings he had given her on their anniversary five years ago. God, how well he remembered making love to her when she was wearing nothing but his gift. It seemed like anything but fair play that she would wear that particular jewelry on this particular day. This was painful enough for both of them as it was.

Megan squared her small shoulders and met Case's frowning gaze evenly.

"I don't need an attorney. I have no intention of getting a divorce," she declared stoutly.

Arnold Bentley's head came up at that. He looked with slightly raised eyebrows from Megan to Case, waiting.

Case glared at Megan, trying to force her to drop her gaze first and acknowledge this opening ploy for the unnecessary show of bravado that it undoubtedly was. How like Megan to want to cause a scene. But she wouldn't look away.

"Let's get on with this," he ordered the attorney in a disgusted tone, transferring his gaze with grim determination to the thick pile of papers in front of Arnold Bentley, who cleared his throat again as though to emphasize his willingness to comply. His fastidious expression along with the excessively polite tone of his voice when he began said that he hoped the other parties present would curb their emotions and conduct themselves with civility for the sake of everyone, including himself.

Megan paid scant attention to the attorney's facts and figures. She kept her eyes on Case, not to make him uncomfortable and not to engage in any further battle of wills through eye contact, but simply because she needed to look at him and reaffirm her certainty that he meant everything to her.

Today, in spite of his grimness, he looked wonderful to her eyes, vigorous and male and *dear*. His dark brown hair was at that unruly stage she liked, just before he got a new haircut and tamed it into submission again. His heavy, full beard was close-trimmed to the square shape of his jaw, the iron gray fast becoming predominant over the sable brown. His tan had faded a little, but he still looked like a Coppertone commercial next to pale Arnold Bentley and herself. Those lines fanning out from the corners of his eyes and those two deep creases between his eyebrows, she didn't remember them as being etched so noticeably.

"Does either of you have a question thus far?" Arnold Bentley had paused to inquire pompously, looking from Case to Megan and back to Case. "No?" He turned over the pages in front of him methodically, looking for one particular document. "Mrs. Ballantine, just to complete the record, I would like to get some information from you so that I can arrive at an estimated income for yourself and the two children. What is your present salary?"

Megan almost gulped with her surprise. The moment she had been nervously awaiting had arrived so unexpectedly. She took a deep breath and dropped her bombshell.

"As of the end of this month, I won't have a salary, Mr. Bentley," she informed him casually. "I no longer will be employed."

"What?" Case ejaculated before the attorney could react. *"Why* won't you have a job? You don't

mean to tell me that Dee Gardner—" His tone hardened and his face was flooded with disgust as he made the reasonable but wrong assumption that Megan had lost her job through some foul play on the part of her aggressive editor-in-chief. "What happened?" he demanded with a foreboding expression. Privately he was resolving that he intended to let Dee Gardner know exactly what he thought of her even if he didn't carry any clout in the fashion field now that he was out of it.

"Dee Gardner had nothing to do with it," Megan assured him hastily. "I quit."

A stunned silence greeted this matter-of-fact revelation.

"You *quit?*" Case repeated incredulously.

Arnold Bentley sighed gently, but the sound went unheard. For all the attention the other two paid him, he might not have been there at the table with them. Somehow he didn't think this business would be concluded today.

"I quit," Megan said again, softly this time. Her voice grew pleading as she continued. "You win, Case. If I have to choose between you and a career—between you and *anything*—I'd rather have you. Nothing means anything if we're not together."

Arnold Bentley coughed, embarrassed. "I'll just give you two a few minutes to talk this out in private," he said politely, closing the folder and getting to his feet.

"Thanks," Case said tersely, flinging him an absent glance.

"You can take that with you and throw it in the

trashcan," Megan told the lawyer recklessly, gesturing toward the thick folder with all its documents written in legalese. "Can't he, Case?" she begged, leaning forward as far as the table would allow and extending her hands across it toward Case. She implored him to agree, using her eyes and her face and her body as well as her voice.

Arnold Bentley quietly left the room.

"Meg—"

The name was torn out of Case, a kind of protest. He wiped one hand roughly across his face in a gesture that bespoke the deep uncertainty that wouldn't allow him to take her hands even though he wanted to touch her. But Megan had heard the yearning in that single syllable.

"I love you, Case," she said softly. "Don't you still love me, too?"

Case uttered a sound part groan and part sigh as he reached for her hands and grasped them in a convulsive squeeze that made Megan wince and listen involuntarily for the snap of bones. But physical pain was inconsequential at a time like this.

"Why are you *doing* this to me?" Case demanded savagely, anger as well as torment burning in his eyes and constricting his face. "You may have quit your job, as you say, but it doesn't change anything, does it? You won't be happy without a career of your own—" He broke off, his teeth clenched with his overwhelming frustration. "Damn it! I thought I'd explained all this the day I came to your office. We can't go *back*, Meg!"

Megan worked her hands gently free of his and

slipped hers on top, massaging his tightly clenched fingers.

"No, we can't," she agreed softly. "Nobody ever can. But as long as we love each other and we're both willing to work at it, why can't we have something even better?" She could see the yearning gain strength in his eyes and his face, but it was mingled with doubts she must somehow override while still being totally honest with him. "Case, I'm not saying to you that I still don't have the need to come up against challenges that will test my intelligence and my capabilities. I have to have something more stimulating out of life than taking courses in Chinese cooking and quilting. But I'll go anywhere with you. And I can promise you that you'll always come first."

Case searched her eyes and found nothing but sincerity in their depths. He wanted terribly to believe her. But the past two and a half years had been sheer hell. He didn't know if he could bear to go through it again. While he didn't doubt that she believed what she was telling him, that their marriage and their relationship would come first, how could he know she wasn't just reacting to an emergency situation in her life? Could she be happy just being his wife after the heady stimulation of being on the editorial staff of one of the best-known women's magazines in the world?

"Meg, I'm definitely getting out of fashion photography," he stated gravely, extricating his hands and withdrawing them several inches away from hers. "The next few years I can't promise you any large income like I've been earning. You'd be taking a chance."

Megan's fingers curled impotently, wanting to follow after his hands, wanting to reconnect the contact of flesh to flesh.

"I *know* you're getting out of fashion photography," she said earnestly. "And I'm *glad*. It makes our chances of rebuilding our marriage even better. Now you won't feel like a martyr to your family. You'll be able to find out whatever it is that you want to do . . . and I can, too. Don't you see that, Case?"

Quite without his knowledge that he had even moved his hands, Case edged them a fraction of an inch toward hers.

"But what is it you want to do?" he asked cautiously. "You've just given up a job you enjoyed and were good at."

Megan knew they had just arrived at the really hazardous stage. Declarations of good intentions were fine, but Case was too much of a realist and he had suffered too deeply not to want something more concrete.

"I can't tell you that specifically any more than you can tell me what *you* want to do," she pointed out bluntly. "You want to do something with a camera, right?" Her eyes interrogated him while she waited with indrawn breath, not nearly as cool inside as she appeared.

Case nodded. "Yes, I do know that much."

"Well, I like journalism." She pursed her lips thoughtfully. "I enjoy writing in general, but when I took all those writing courses several years ago, I found I was much better at nonfiction than fiction. My imagination is the kind that needs a concrete stimulus, some event or person or place or thing." Eagerness overcame her caution. "Actually, we couldn't ask for two more compatible interests, could we, Case?" she demanded, wondering if he saw all the possibilities that she saw for the two of them working together. "The great thing about photography *and* journalism is that you don't have to be tied down to one place," she rushed on, encouraged that even if he didn't look convinced, he was listening closely.

"We could both do freelance work until we found some place we really liked and wanted to settle permanently." A thought struck suddenly, bringing a cloud to her face. "Here I've completely forgotten the kids. We have to consider them . . . school and their friends . . ."

"That's right," Case put in sternly. "They're getting to an age now where we couldn't be pulling them up every few months or even every year and moving them somewhere else, especially when it's not necessary."

Megan's heart plummeted at the *we* and then rose and began beating triple time. She didn't dare speak. If Case's fatherly instincts worked in her favor, she was only the more grateful.

"I have a project in mind that I could do where we are now as well as anywhere else. Maybe even better," he began hesitantly. "A book on fashion photography. I've been approached on the subject by publishers several times the last few years."

Megan's heart took off for the ceiling at this news, but she controlled the impulse to blurt out the hope that trembled in her breast: She could help Case with a project like that.

"There's another possibility that's more of a long-shot deal," Case was continuing, his voice no longer tentative but confident now. His eyes had brightened with enthusiasm as though life was no longer such a grim prospect.

"What is it?" Megan breathed, forcing herself to stay in her seat, a discipline that required no little effort.

"I've been taking pictures to please myself for all these years. Random shots of people and places wherever I happened to be with a camera in my hands. Pictures of you and the kids, too, pictures of the city, pictures of work and play, happiness and sadness. There's a whole filing cabinet full of them at the studio. In the back of my mind, I always intended to go through them someday and pick out the best ones . . ." He shrugged, giving the first indication that he would like some response from her, perhaps some encouragement and reinforcement, she divined.

"I'd love to go through them with you," she ventured timidly and then gave into her enthusiasm when she saw that her suggestion pleased him. "Oh, Case, I'd love to work with you on those two projects . . . or on *anything!* We made a great team on the Caribbean feature, even with all the personal problems that interfered. I admire your work so much—"

Megan was about to breach the small space separating their hands, but suddenly the glossy surface of the table was more distance between them than she could tolerate. She had to touch more of him than his hands. She *had* to feel his arms around her.

Murmuring his name aloud, she popped up out of the chair and made her way around the table toward him. The journey proved to be only half as long as she had expected, since Case came part of the way himself. They met at Arnold Bentley's chair. Case closed his arms around her with a groan that came from deep inside him. Holding her close against him, he reveled in the tightness of her arms around his neck.

"Do you really think it'll work this time, Meg, darling?" he begged roughly, the words welling out of the longing that filled his insides.

"I know it will! It *has* to!" she promised him tenderly.

For a long moment they wanted nothing but to cling to each other and bask in the miracle of being together, *really* together, after such an interminable separation, one that had begun, they both realized now, before Megan had defied Case and he had moved out of the house. They had begun to drift apart earlier.

"Do you love me, Case?" Megan asked wistfully, tilting her head back to look up into his face. She wanted the words to reinforce what his arms were telling her.

His dark eyes were alight with the answer and fiercely possessive as he plumbed her gaze.

"You know I do. Even when I hated you, I loved you."

"I know *exactly* what you mean!" Megan cried, all aglow with joy.

Case dragged Mr. Bentley's chair farther out into the room and sat down on it, pulling Megan down onto his lap. He cradled her close, stroking her hair and gently pressing her face into his shoulder. The happiness inside him was growing steadily, spreading warmth through his entire body.

"I can't wait to move back into the house." His low voice vibrated with anticipation. "You were right when you said I loved that house, but it's more than that. It's going to be so great living with you and the kids again. . . . You don't know how much I missed all the little things. Eating our meals together, looking in on the kids when they were asleep in their beds at night, going to bed with you and waking up with you in the morning . . ." Case had to stop, overwhelmed by his emotion.

Megan wanted to cry. To rescue the situation from becoming even more painful to them both, she swallowed the lump in her throat and managed a chuckle.

"There're some new 'little things' I can't wait to share with you," she said wryly, the words muffled against his chest. "Like the telephone ringing every fifteen minutes for your little girl, who has a boyfriend these days. And lately Danny's been setting new records for the time it can take to get thirty minutes' worth of math homework done."

Case squeezed her tighter.

"I can't wait," he said huskily, a smile in his voice.

Megan struggled against the tight band of his arms. "Why don't we go straight to your apartment and get your things packed up?" she suggested eagerly.

Case loosened his hold and let her sit up. As her eyes met his she saw something new in them that quickened her pulse.

"I'm definitely for going straight to my apartment," he agreed suggestively, letting his gaze touch her parted lips before it dropped to her breasts, which thrust forward a fraction of an inch more in instinctive invitation.

"Sex. That's all you men think of," she declared with pretended disapproval, clicking her tongue and then undermining her words by lightly caressing his face with her fingertips. She offered no resistance when he cupped the back of her head with one hand and brought her lips to his.

The kiss was gentle but hungry at first as they shared with each other the need that had been built up over the weeks of separation. Then the gentleness was swallowed up by the hunger.

When the door to the conference room opened quietly, Mr. Bentley's secretary saw two people kissing each other as though they would never stop, their lips meshing and their heads turning from side to side as though they sought to consume each other. She couldn't fail to notice, either, that Mr. Ballantine's hands were *everywhere*. After observing the scene longer than necessary, Ms. McCormack closed the door once again and went to her employer's office to report that it was highly unlikely his conference with the Ballantines would be resumed that day.

Mr. Bentley wasn't surprised. "The folder," he reminded, rising from the richly upholstered chair behind his desk. He might as well make an early day of it. "I left all the documents we prepared for Mr. Ballantine in the conference room. Did you get it?"

"Er, no," Ms. McCormack replied discreetly. "I'll get it *later*."

Mr. Bentley caught her delicate emphasis and noted the heightened color in her cheeks. He nodded once, knowingly.

"I see." He became occupied loading up his briefcase. "Well, whenever you can, get it and put it here on my desk. We'll wait for further instructions from Mr. Ballantine. One way or the other, we'll keep the file."

Ms. McCormack acquiesced with a sage smile, knowing as her employer did that a passionate reconciliation was not necessarily of long duration.

But when Ms. McCormack left Mr. Bentley's office and passed by the conference room on the way to her own office, she discovered that the door to the conference room was open. The Ballantines must have come to themselves long enough to realize they should seek a more suitable place to continue their "discussion." But lo and behold, when Ms. McCormack looked for the folder, it was gone!

Unbeknown to her, the quiet click of the door closing had been audible to Case and Megan several minutes earlier in spite of their absorption in each other. Case had lightened his pressure on Megan's mouth just enough to mutter indistinctly, "Let's get the hell out of here."

"Let's," Megan had agreed with an involuntary shiver of passion.

Case stood up with her in his arms and slowly let her body slide against his until she stood on her own two feet. The sensual contact heightened their arousal until Case was halfway tempted to lock the damned door and make love to her right there on the carpet. Megan saw the impulse in his face and pulled reluctantly away from him.

"Let's go to your apartment," she urged softly. "I can't wait to have you make love to me . . . and I want it to be perfect, the way it was down in the islands. Case, remember the night I sneaked into your stateroom?"

The question was purely rhetorical. As Case's eyes met hers they shared the highly provocative memory of their passion that night their bodies had joined for the first time in two long years.

"Let's go," Case said abruptly, grabbing her arm and propelling her toward the door.

"Wait—"

Megan balked, pulling against him. Case frowned down at her in puzzlement and then watched as she reached toward the conference table and took the thick legal-sized folder.

"What do you want with that?"

"I'm going to destroy it," she declared with grim determination. With the folder under one arm she linked the other in his. "Ready?"

"But why do you want to destroy it?" Case inquired in a stage whisper as they left the room, as though he were a partner in crime.

"Because I don't want it stuck in some file somewhere," she whispered back fiercely, urging him to go faster when they were in the hallway.

In keeping with the spirit of intrigue, neither of them spoke as they hurriedly retrieved their overcoats from the closet in the outer office. When they had gained the safety of the elevator, Case enfolded her with one arm and expelled his breath in mock relief.

"Looks like we may have gotten away with the 'goods,' partner," he teased. Then curiosity got the best of him. "Seriously, Meg, why do you want to destroy those papers? What difference does it make if Bentley *does* stick them in some filing cabinet?"

"Well, he *won't*," Megan insisted strongly, clinging tighter to the folder. It was hard for her to explain, but she just knew she had to destroy every shred of evidence that she and Case had come this perilously close to divorce. "It would be wasted space," she added in the same fierce tone. "Because you might as well get one thing straight, Case Ballantine. You're never getting a divorce from me. You can spend every cent you own hiring lawyers to draw up hateful papers, and I'll just tear them up."

Case heard the hint of tears behind the protective bluster and understood. He hugged her closer, folder and all, and pressed a kiss against the top of her head.

"As soon as we get to the apartment, I'll help you shred those papers to smithereens," he promised warmly as the elevator doors slid noiselessly open and he walked out into the future with his wife.

Silhouette Special Edition

MORE ROMANCE FOR
A SPECIAL WAY TO RELAX
$1.95 each

2 ☐ Hastings	21 ☐ Hastings	41 ☐ Halston	60 ☐ Thorne
3 ☐ Dixon	22 ☐ Howard	42 ☐ Drummond	61 ☐ Beckman
4 ☐ Vitek	23 ☐ Charles	43 ☐ Shaw	62 ☐ Bright
5 ☐ Converse	24 ☐ Dixon	44 ☐ Eden	63 ☐ Wallace
6 ☐ Douglass	25 ☐ Hardy	45 ☐ Charles	64 ☐ Converse
7 ☐ Stanford	26 ☐ Scott	46 ☐ Howard	65 ☐ Cates
8 ☐ Halston	27 ☐ Wisdom	47 ☐ Stephens	66 ☐ Mikels
9 ☐ Baxter	28 ☐ Ripy	48 ☐ Ferrell	67 ☐ Shaw
10 ☐ Thiels	29 ☐ Bergen	49 ☐ Hastings	68 ☐ Sinclair
11 ☐ Thornton	30 ☐ Stephens	50 ☐ Browning	69 ☐ Dalton
12 ☐ Sinclair	31 ☐ Baxter	51 ☐ Trent	70 ☐ Clare
13 ☐ Beckman	32 ☐ Douglass	52 ☐ Sinclair	71 ☐ Skillern
14 ☐ Keene	33 ☐ Palmer	53 ☐ Thomas	72 ☐ Belmont
15 ☐ James	35 ☐ James	54 ☐ Hohl	73 ☐ Taylor
16 ☐ Carr	36 ☐ Dailey	55 ☐ Stanford	74 ☐ Wisdom
17 ☐ John	37 ☐ Stanford	56 ☐ Wallace	75 ☐ John
18 ☐ Hamilton	38 ☐ John	57 ☐ Thornton	76 ☐ Ripy
19 ☐ Shaw	39 ☐ Milan	58 ☐ Douglass	77 ☐ Bergen
20 ☐ Musgrave	40 ☐ Converse	59 ☐ Roberts	78 ☐ Gladstone

$2.25 each

79 ☐ Hastings	87 ☐ Dixon	95 ☐ Doyle	103 ☐ Taylor
80 ☐ Douglass	88 ☐ Saxon	96 ☐ Baxter	104 ☐ Wallace
81 ☐ Thornton	89 ☐ Meriwether	97 ☐ Shaw	105 ☐ Sinclair
82 ☐ McKenna	90 ☐ Justin	98 ☐ Hurley	106 ☐ John
83 ☐ Major	91 ☐ Stanford	99 ☐ Dixon	107 ☐ Ross
84 ☐ Stephens	92 ☐ Hamilton	100 ☐ Roberts	108 ☐ Stephens
85 ☐ Beckman	93 ☐ Lacey	101 ☐ Bergen	109 ☐ Beckman
86 ☐ Halston	94 ☐ Barrie	102 ☐ Wallace	110 ☐ Browning

Silhouette Special Edition

$2.25 each

111 ☐ Thorne	128 ☐ Macomber	145 ☐ Wallace	162 ☐ Roberts
112 ☐ Belmont	129 ☐ Rowe	146 ☐ Thornton	163 ☐ Halston
113 ☐ Camp	130 ☐ Carr	147 ☐ Dalton	164 ☐ Ripy
114 ☐ Ripy	131 ☐ Lee	148 ☐ Gordon	165 ☐ Lee
115 ☐ Halston	132 ☐ Dailey	149 ☐ Claire	166 ☐ John
116 ☐ Roberts	133 ☐ Douglass	150 ☐ Dailey	167 ☐ Hurley
117 ☐ Converse	134 ☐ Ripy	151 ☐ Shaw	168 ☐ Thornton
118 ☐ Jackson	135 ☐ Seger	152 ☐ Adams	
119 ☐ Langan	136 ☐ Scott	153 ☐ Sinclair	
120 ☐ Dixon	137 ☐ Parker	154 ☐ Malek	
121 ☐ Shaw	138 ☐ Thornton	155 ☐ Lacey	
122 ☐ Walker	139 ☐ Halston	156 ☐ Hastings	
123 ☐ Douglass	140 ☐ Sinclair	157 ☐ Taylor	
124 ☐ Mikels	141 ☐ Saxon	158 ☐ Charles	
125 ☐ Cates	142 ☐ Bergen	159 ☐ Camp	
126 ☐ Wildman	143 ☐ Bright	160 ☐ Wisdom	
127 ☐ Taylor	144 ☐ Meriwether	161 ☐ Stanford	

SILHOUETTE SPECIAL EDITION, Department SE/2
1230 Avenue of the Americas
New York, NY 10020

Please send me the books I have checked above. I am enclosing $_____
(please add 75¢ to cover postage and handling. NYS and NYC residents please
add appropriate sales tax). Send check or money order—no cash or C.O.D.'s
please. Allow six weeks for delivery.

NAME _____

ADDRESS _____

CITY _____ STATE/ZIP _____

MAIL THIS COUPON
and get 4 thrilling
Silhouette Desire®
novels **FREE** (a $7.80 value)

Silhouette Desire books may not be for everyone. They *are* for readers who want a sensual, provocative romance. These are modern love stories that are charged with emotion from the first page to the thrilling happy ending—about women who discover the extremes of fiery passion. Confident women who face the challenge of today's world and overcome all obstacles to attain their dreams—*and their desires*.

We believe you'll be so delighted with Silhouette Desire romance novels that you'll want to receive them regularly through our home subscription service. Your books will be *shipped to you two months before they're available anywhere else*—so you'll never miss a new title. Each month we'll send you 6 new books to look over for 15 days, without obligation. If not delighted, simply return them and owe nothing. Or keep them and pay only $1.95 each. There's no charge for postage or handling. And there's no obligation to buy anything at any time. You'll also receive a subscription to the Silhouette Books Newsletter *absolutely free!*

So don't wait. To receive your four FREE books, fill out and mail the coupon below *today!*

SILHOUETTE DESIRE and colophon are registered trademarks and a service mark of Simon & Schuster, Inc

---

Silhouette Desire,® 120 Brighton Road, P.O. Box 5020, Clifton, NJ 07015

Yes, please send me FREE and without obligation, 4 exciting Silhouette Desire books. Unless you hear from me after I receive them, send me 6 new Silhouette Desire books to preview each month before they're available anywhere else. I understand that you will bill me just $1.95 each for a total of $11.70—with no additional shipping, handling or other hidden charges. **There is no minimum number of books that I must buy, and I can cancel anytime I wish.** The first 4 books are mine to keep, even if I never take a single additional book.

☐ Mrs. ☐ Miss ☐ Ms. ☐ Mr.   **BDS5R4**

Name		*(please print)*	
Address			Apt. #
City		State	Zip
( )			
Area Code	Telephone Number		

Signature (If under 18, parent or guardian must sign.)

This offer, limited to one per customer, expires November 30, 1984. Terms and prices subject to change. Your enrollment is subject to acceptance by Simon & Schuster Enterprises.

Silhouette Special Edition

Coming Next Month

Storm Over The Everglades by Patti Beckman

Lindi MacTavish agreed to handle her family's newspaper in Florida, but she soon found she wasn't able to handle brooding Travis Machado, the paper's mysterious managing editor.

Lover's Choice by Laurie Paige

Meli wanted a husband, and Tor offered to help her find one. But how could he follow through with his plan when his burning kisses told her he never planned to let her go?

Golden Illusion by Ginna Gray

Claire Andrews was determined not to be a figurehead senator. She fought to show Matt Drummond that she was cool and capable, but soon she couldn't hide the explosive passion only he aroused.

Shooting Star by Lucy Hamilton

When Cassie, a resident in obstetrics, met movie star James Reid, their attraction was immediate and deep. But how could their love survive when their lives were on such different paths?

From The Flames by Kathryn Belmont

Full of humor and passion, Jack Clancy drove away the loneliness that had haunted widow Marie Russo's nights. But the mystery surrounding her fireman husband's death threatened to destroy them both.

No Strings by Diana Dixon

Used to women who put a price on everything, Christian was unable to believe that Allana would offer her love freely. But as she painted his portrait Allana captured his soul—and his heart.